Unmapped

An Anthology

Volume 2 of the SMITHworks Writing Group

Also by the SMITHworks Writing Group
17 Secrets

Unmapped

An Anthology

Edited by Rebecca M. Zornow

Table of Contents

Editor's Note

The first meeting of the SMITHworks Writing Group was hosted on February 14, 2022. Perhaps Valentine's Day was not the ideal date on which to found a social creative group, and indeed there were only two in attendance. The ratio of facilitator to attendee was one-to-one.

The following March, there were four writers, April nine, and we grew from there. It's not uncommon for me to go running out of the conference room for more chairs in the moments before the session begins.

Once in the Gegan Room, where we typically meet, the old, corded phone rang just as we were starting. Everyone looked around at each other, and I answered it with some trepidation. It was one of the librarians calling from the floor above to say someone new was on their way down to attend for the first time. That individual never showed up. Whether it was nerves or they are still lost in the Elisha D. Smith Public Library, I can't say.

But of those who do show up, and continuously, I can say are well rewarded. It is only the writer that comes to the page often, that sets aside doubt or fear to create, that grows.

As a book coach, I meet a lot of writers, a lot of aspiring authors. I can say with confidence the number one thing that keeps a writer from writing, from success, from creativity, is themselves.

The writers featured in *Unmapped* range across various stages of the writing journey. Some are established, published authors. For others, their story in this collection is their first published piece. All are embarking on a new frontier. They experiment and trial new methods of writing, spin new thoughts and ideas to put down on the page.

We chose frontiers as the theme of this collection because it lends so much creative opportunity. Any writer in any genre—non-fiction, poetry, sci-fi, romance—has something to say about a new frontier. You'll find stories that span genre, length, and technique in this collection.

The idea of the frontier is also a staple of the writing journey. There is always a new frontier to explore of one's creative mind, of one's ability to construct plot and weave dialogue, even of business and process.

I want to congratulate each of the thirteen writers in this collection who not only wrote their own stories, but peer edited each other's work, chose the title and cover, formatted the manuscript, built a book launch plan, and continually gave "just one more proof."

Thank you for going on this journey with us into a new frontier.

Rebecca M. Zornow
Author & Book Coach
ConquerBooks.com

Contributors

DON BRITTNACHER writes with humor about the mishaps that occur when people try to outwit life. His stories reveal the beauty of common experiences when viewed with curiosity. Don and his wife Chris live in Northeastern Wisconsin and enjoy family and outdoor silent sports. He can be reached at dbrittnacher@new.rr.com.

SYLVIA COOPMAN tends to write from the perspective of objects rather than live beings and she is still exploring her writing style. She is a graduating senior at Menasha High School (2024) and will be attending St. Cloud State University in the fall. This is her first publication and she is excited to continue her writing career. She enjoys quiet, late nights, and the sound of nature.

DANNA DIETZ has been writing poetry and non-fiction since she was a young teenager. She has worked in healthcare for over a decade now, keeping her on her toes, but yet still grounded. She illustrates real-life experiences through her understanding and utmost honesty; a mix between dark, witty, and cheerful humor. She is aspiring to be uplifting and hopeful for others who are channeling through their own trauma and struggles. Danna resides in the Menasha area, and is extremely grateful for this opportunity to work with other talented, local authors to fulfil her dream of becoming a published author as well.

MAX DEMAY writes stories with LGBTQIA+ themes. Between rock-climbing, choir, and writing group, he still finds time seven days a week to think about the Roman Empire. Check his Goodreads to see his opinions on everyone from Colleen Hoover to Herman Melville. Follow on Instagram @max_demay.

DON FAHRENKRUG is an author of poetry and short stories typically involving subjects of relationships, nature, and thought provoking situations. He writes with the hope of change towards a better understanding of acceptance within us. Please relax and enjoy the work from the authors in this collection.

S.J. HEINZ studied journalism. These are her first attempts at writing science fiction. She recently discovered the joy of watercolor. You are invited to join in her journeys on Facebook at Ageless Art, WORD Whistle, and the Menasha Historical Society.

K. L. MIELKE is a Menasha graduate and a fantasy-romance author. She has five anthologies and six novels out (most available on Amazon). She is honored to be part of this collection and encourages writers at any point in the creative process to reach out and find a supportive community. Find her at Facebook @KLMielkeAuthor, Instagram @klmielke_author, and TikTok @klmielkeauthor.

ERIC REUTER is a writer of fantasy and adventure stories. This experience has been truly rewarding and he's proud to publish alongside many talented individuals from the Fox Valley. He hopes to share more of his stories someday. When he's not busy writing, he loves spending time with his wife and sons.

LORI O'BRIAN SMITH is a Fox Valley native. She has lived in the Philadelphia area, Hawaii, and now in Neenah. You can find her first book *Madam President* on Amazon. Writing and watercolor painting are retirement pursuits.

RYAN SURPRISE is a historical fiction writer and author of the western novel, *Stories of a Hangman*. He received his BA at Carroll University. He is a Wisconsin-based writer who loves exploring the natural beauty of the Northern Midwest, currently living in his hometown of Appleton.

ELIZABETH WESTENBERGER is a writer from Appleton, Wisconsin. She spends most of her time studying Professional Communications and attempting to escape from a pile of unread books and manga. She hopes everyone can find a story they can relate to, or one that can help them escape for a little while.

CYNTHIA SEIDL WITT loves to read and write a good story. After working as a communications professional for more than 20 years, she is just rediscovering creative writing. Her favorite genre is historical fiction, but she also enjoys dabbling in science fiction and fantasy. Favorite pastimes include traveling, adventuring, and spending time with family.

REBECCA M. ZORNOW is a Hal Prize winner, member of the Science Fiction and Fantasy Writers Association, and graduate of Lawrence University. She is the author of *It's Over or It's Eden, Dangerous to Heal*, and *Negotiated Fate*, and supports writers as a book coach specializing in speculative fiction. Sign up for her newsletter at RebeccaMZornow.com.

What Whispers Within

Elizabeth Westenberger

The wilderness had control before we decided to take it. The dark pines reached for the sky. Thorny vines stretched across the forest floor, unchecked, until civilization began to fight back.

We advanced, raising buildings from the ground overnight; claiming a small clearing in the forest and expanding like weeds. Over time, the trees disappeared, replaced by snaking cobblestone paths. We villagers lived blissful lives but the beings living between the trees did not. And no wonder, we never treated them kindly. We chopped the snaking vines without so much as a second thought. We never cared about how they felt. But looking back, I know they held out for one thing and the bliss we enjoyed wouldn't last long.

As we expanded our own little world, we got brave. As kids, we would tease each other through the village, testing how far we could go. The older citizens always wanted more: land, resources, control. They didn't care what it took to get it. For years the forest would gain its strength only for us to steal it. Make no mistake, I know exactly what I've done. And with the way the world is now, I would take it all back if I could.

Nothing could get in our way. We defeated the insects, we even stood our ground against the predators who called the wilderness home. We tore our way through not realizing there was more under the surface of trees. Like the moon and its phases, the wild and civilized grappled with one rising above the other until we ultimately had our way. The flora wilted but this wasn't the end.

Something dark lurked deep within the pines. It was hard to detect drifting through the air but it sometimes spoke through flowers and fungi, vines and moss. It turned life into monotonous shades of gray, pulling the energy from everything in its wake. It came out of hiding, knowing it was the only thing that could keep the woodland and everything in it safe.

My hunting party would come out at sunrise. Laughing with each other, we mused over all of the treasures we would bring home. We did this for years until something shifted and changed everything. As we moved through the forest a static would overwhelm us; keeping us suspended between silence and stifling noise. Always quiet but hard to ignore. No one liked it but still we pressed on, not wanting our families to think of us as weak.

We complained about our heads feeling heavy as if stuffed with fabric but we wouldn't leave. We moved slowly, but continued to take what wasn't ours.

By the time the sun hung low in the sky, some of the people in our group would slump to the ground and even fewer wanted to get back up. They spoke of a weight suddenly pressing down on them, not too heavy to handle, but persistent enough to drain every bit of energy we had. Through it all we did return home. But we didn't show off our menial prizes. We didn't tell stories of the giant animals we hunted out in the wilderness. All the affected ones wanted to do was retreat to their beds.

A new kind of weed was spreading. It had no thorns or no flowers. No one could see it with their eyes but we could sense it. It wouldn't slink in right away but we would all be afflicted. The static filled the village. The stuffy feelings in our heads loomed over us like dark clouds over a storm and the weight got harder to bear each day. At first, nothing could get in the way of our civilization in its infancy. But it wasn't long until it all became too much for us. No more buildings rose and no one stepped beyond the bounds of the wilderness. Everyone lived on but nothing was the same once the forest decided to fight back.

Fine China and Thieves

K.L. Mielke

Despite its darker reputation, few residents of Acies knew that The Broken Mirror Saloon served the best coffee in town. The owner, Mors, was among the few vampires who worked after sunrise, tending the bar until his employees took over. Known for nights of serving secret elixirs and dining with demons, few knew that the display shelf behind the bar of colorful China pieces was more than decor. It was something of an obsession for the soft-spoken owner. Fewer still knew he often stored his extra magic in his most treasured fragile pitchers and ornate gravy boats. Having seen them as they made their way to the vault at the bank where I worked, I could appreciate his good taste.

Mors slid a pink teacup across the bar where I sat, the same cup he gave me every morning. He then resumed drying the dainty cups and platters he'd used the night before, putting them just so in their place of honor on the shelf behind the bar. "Doris," he said solemnly, "you're looking well."

My laugh was more of a harrumph. His reputation also preceded his humor. "Looking well" was saved for those under the age of thirty who might provide his next meal. His daily comment about my features had become a joke between friends, and served as a reminder that I was not his target demographic when it came to blood. Too acidic, he told me once. The idea of our bodies souring as we aged had always humored me.

I'd been coming to The Broken Mirror for breakfast for decades. I knew not to question what occupied my cup before the coffee, hoping the heat of the liquid would scorch away the remnants of whatever was in it the night before, when the furious or most desperate of visitors chanced a meeting with a powerful vampire. Mornings were ruined if I dwelled on their sorry souls.

"Morning, Doris."

I nodded at Domina, the elf who passed behind Mors with a large wooden barrel. She was sunshine personified, dismissing Mors' quiet demeanor with a kiss on his cheek as she headed to the stockroom. The only reaction from her husband was the color creeping up Mors' neck as he continued to dry. The pair had been together for over a century, and while she was nearly two hundred years old, Domina looked no older than twenty. I envied her genetics, having inherited my mother's chin hair and only managing to hide my father's receding hairline with elf hair serum and stubborn determination.

"Working today?" Mors asked me as he reached for another cup.

I nodded, sipping the dark roast. Cinnamon was banned from The Broken Mirror Saloon due to the blood-drinkers' delicate palettes. Instead, the coffee was sweetened with caramel and sugar. Slowly, my eyes sharpened and my soul warmed as only hot, caffeinated beverages could do.

My shift started in twenty minutes, but I wouldn't be late. I liked my job at the bank. Without it, my life would be painfully monotonous. It allowed me to creature-watch in a way that didn't involve gambling, drinking, or any other ruinous or nefarious acts. Save that for the young and foolish. Goodness knew they came in droves to visit Acies, the town on the edge of civilization.

The saloon was slow in the mornings. A group of three people sat in one corner. Humans, I decided, as they gawked with fearful eyes at the body of a woman covered in pairs of puncture marks on the floor. They huddled together over a large pitcher of coffee. As they sipped, their gray hairs dissolved and their shoulders began to straighten.

"Youth serum," Mors said when he caught me watching. "I can get you some if you'd like. On the house for my best customer."

I huffed a laugh. "No, thank you." He'd offered several of Domina's concoctions to me in the past, but I always refused. Humans had no business using magic or any of the like. Magic wielders had lifetimes of practice using what they'd been given at birth, while humans' craving for magic stemmed from feelings of greed and desperation for power. I'd seen enough in my life to know that magic, in the wrong hands, was catastrophic. The elf serum was the only exception. A girl did what she had to do to prevent her head from looking like an egg.

Leaving a few gold coins on the bar—silver wasn't allowed at the saloon either—I stood with a groan. Dust covered the floors and settled deep in my bones. I gathered my ivory cane that doubled as a weapon as well as a walking stick, and stepped around the body. A pretty young brunette in the remnants of a red silk dress slumped against the wall, lying as though she'd wilted like a dried flower. Her skin was so pale it was nearly blue. I swallowed my shudder, blocking the reality from my mind. There were rules, of course, but in a town like Acies, the authorities were overworked, underpaid, and too few to hammer down order in the chaos.

"My apologies, Doris," Mors called. "I'll have that cleaned up right away."

I waved without looking back at him, not dwelling on what "cleaning up" meant. Minding my own business kept me alive this far. I wasn't going to jeopardize my future by asking prying questions or quoting the rules.

Outside, the morning air was sticky hot. Three forest nymphs skipped by arm in arm as I emerged, giggling in falsetto. I rolled my eyes. Of all the magic wielders that came into Acies, the forest nymphs were amongst the most ridiculous. Their magic was short-lived outside the forest, and Acies was too busy drowning in construction to keep more than a piddly bush or two outside storefronts. The nymphs would need to return to the forest every fortnight to replenish, or get their magic from the bank. And I didn't recognize any of them as clients.

My final stop of the morning, The Bona Bank, stood at the edge of town. Steps beyond the edge of the building, large dunes of sand lined the worn road. Strange cacti grew like a den of mangled, twisted snakes clawing high into the sky. On cooler days, I'd see dragons and other strange beings soaring over the dunes. On the hottest, a bright blue fire danced over the sands, consuming nothing in its path.

Beyond its location to the magical wilderness, Bona was unassuming. Like its neighbors, the facade was painted in jewel tones, with bars on the windows flanked by wooden shutters. It lacked the front porch of the other buildings, a subtle dissuasion from loitering. The large ornate doors kept most of the dust and dirt out and the cool air in. In agreement with keeping their magic stored safely, clients and customers donated a bit of their magic to keep the environment a decent place for employees to spend the day. With age causing certain parts to soften, sag, and ache constantly, this job beat pushing whiskey or cleaning rooms. I'd go to work with the dwarves in the mines before forcing myself into tight corsets and short skirts to sell liquor to the Acies underbelly.

The tellers each had their designated stalls. I ambled into mine, breathing in the musty pine. Three stacks of slips, a cup of pencils, and not a speck of dust or dirt. Neat and organized, the way I liked it.

"Good morning, Doris."

"Morning, Trixie." The stall to my right was the opposite of mine in every way. Flowers filled vases flanking the window, and dried herbs hung on the walls. While she wasn't a registered witch, I'd seen Trixie practicing small spells when we weren't busy. Her specialty was turning flowers into food. Bubbly women weren't my preferred company either, but Trixie had won me over with her kind personality. Well, that and her mint chocolate cookies.

"How was your night?" she asked, leaning over the counter between us. I feared for the ties on the corset that barely contained her ample bosom. There were rules about proper attire in the bank, but Trixie generally ignored them.

"Same as usual." I sighed when she waited expectantly. "How was yours?"

"Last night at The Broken Mirror, the vampires had a feast on…well, you know…a young lady. Turns out, her brother is in town. He's a filthy rich cattle baron, and he's furious."

I thought about the body I'd stepped over this morning. "It's not good to be out at nighttime, rounding up gossip."

Her blue eyes went wide and her jowls wobbled as she shook her head. "I was working at Ebrius Saloon last night. News jumped down the street faster than the blue dune fires."

"Either way, it's best to keep to yourself."

She leaned in further. "Rumor has it, the brother wants Mors' head on a spike." She shivered. "That's putting what he really said nicely."

There it was. The bank paid well enough, but Trixie insisted on working at the saloon, mainly for the gossip. "People enter The Broken Mirror Saloon willingly," I reminded her. "Mors doesn't take anyone in without their consent," I reminded her.

Trixie shrugged as the guard unlocked the doors to welcome the first customers. "That isn't the story her brother is telling."

"Like I said. Mouth shut, head down. If he has a problem with the goings on at The Broken Mirror Saloon, he'd do well to go to Mors himself."

She nodded as a couple with long, gossamer wings approached her window. "You're not wrong, but grief can make people do crazy things," she said before turning to them with a wide smile.

I nodded to the gnome who headed toward my window, using the step stool to reach the counter. Our job revolved around the exchange of valued items. A few humans kept money in the vaults, gambling that their wealth was safest surrounded by magic. More often, however, the items heading to the vault were similar to the gnome's ruby, which was the shape of a mushroom. It shimmered and warmed beneath my touch. He filled out the appropriate deposit slip and signed it in his short, scratchy writing, eyeing the troll who waited behind him with suspicious disdain. I waved down a courier pigeon to take the gnome's treasure to the vaults. The birds were enchanted to know the contents of the magicked paper and get each piece to its perfect location.

Just after lunch, I was wiping the remnants of a crusty, waterlogged stump from an ogre's withdrawal from my counter when a man approached my window, slapping a sheet of paper down on the counter between us.

I paused, swallowing my irritation at the rude behavior before resuming my cleaning, avoiding the folded page. "Welcome to Bona. May I help you?"

"The note has all of my information," came a low, gruff voice.

With a grunt, I retrieved the waste basket, brushing the remaining bark and dirt into it before finally raising my gaze. A man stood before me, his head low so the hood of his cape covered all of his face except his chin, which was darkened by a few days' worth of hair.

I folded my hands in front of me. "Your voice works fine, so I hear."

"Read the note." The man was jittery, his fingers alternating between fidgeting on the counter and gripping the edge with white knuckles.

I kept my hands folded and waited a moment before responding. "No."

"What do you mean, no?" he demanded.

"Those aren't the bank sheets we use," I said, gesturing to his still-folded note. "Would you like a withdrawal or a deposit slip?"

He shifted, his hands fisting on the edge of the counter before he reached over to flip the note open. Mors' name and business information was scrolled across it. "I want the magic artifacts belonging to the owner of The Broken Mirror Saloon," he said.

"A withdrawal slip, then."

My calm frazzled him. He glanced up then. He was a handsome young man, but his white face was etched with dark bags under his wild blue eyes. Desperation contorted his features, giving him a haggard appearance. "What? No, I'm trying to rob this place."

I pulled one of the blue slips from my pile and slid it across the table, placing a pencil on top. "No, you're not. Now, fill out this sheet."

He reached for the pencil before snapping back. "I'm trying to rob–" he took a deep breath and leaned in closer, lowering his voice. "Get me Mors' artifacts, or I'll—"

"Son," I began, cutting him off with a heavy sigh, "the pigeons are demons in disguise. My neighbor teller is a witch who excels in explosives. She practices when it's slow and keeps it all under her desk. I am armed with six knives you won't see until they're buried in your guts, and my cane is hollow and filled with mephitis, an odorous gas that can kill those who inhale it. The bell under my desk summons the two guards at the door, the troll guarding the vault, and any dragons within a mile radius. Either fill out my slip, or leave."

The man's hands fisted. "Mors killed my sister."

I remembered the body on the floor at The Broken Mirror Saloon. Pity clashed with indifference as I recalled the woman's beautiful brown hair and her pretty dress. "My condolences. But you'll not get your revenge here through me. Perhaps you might speak with Mors himself. Get yourself a cup of coffee, it's quite good." I reached across and patted his hand. "Grief has made you reckless and foolish, son. With time, you'll see that this plan will get you nowhere. Run along now, I've got a line waiting."

For a moment, he simply stared at me, dumbfounded. Then, his eyes narrowed. I wrapped my fingers around my cane, ready to defend myself, but he snatched up the letter and stormed out of the building.

I let out a low whistle of relief. Preventing robberies was easy enough when the would-be thief was a gullible human.

"'All dragons within a mile radius?'" Trixie said with a snort of laughter. "Your pan-faced improvisational skills are unparalleled, Doris."

"It's why they've kept me on payroll so long," I replied as a centaur stepped forward.

Two hours later, a thin, pale-faced man with a wide brimmed hat and dark clothing arrived at my counter. "Compliments of The Broken Mirror Saloon, Ms. Doris," he said, passing me a tall pink floral pitcher and matching teacup through the window.

"Thank you, Adat. Tell Mors I'll return his china in the morning."

He nodded once and left. I poured myself a mug of steaming coffee before passing the jug to Trixie, who squealed with delight and insisted on conjuring blueberry pastries to go with it. They were still a bit dry, but miles better than the bricks she'd concocted the week before.

"To what do we owe the treat?" Trixie asked. I arched a brow at her over my glass and her eyes widened. "That thief! He entered the saloon willingly, didn't he?"

"I did suggest he do so, didn't I?" I shrugged, giving her a small smirk. "It must have gone well."

Rose-Colored Glasses

Cynthia Seidl Witt

The soft, corkscrew curls on Dara's two-year-old head slid forward as she leaned over and finally drifted off to sleep along with her nine-month-old sister, Deena. I clicked the seatbelt closed and tucked her blanket and teddy bear in next to her as we began our 90-minute trek to Washington National Airport, just outside D.C. Nestled in the backseat of our used 1969 Ford Falcon, the girls looked like tiny mahogany-colored angels, gently cushioned on both sides by overstuffed pillows. I sat in between them, white, plump, and pregnant.

My husband, Sam, gripped the steering wheel and focused intently on the road. I was exhausted, crampy, and full of foreboding at what lay ahead. Still, we had to push on.

"They're out," I whispered loudly, trying not to wake the children. He looked back and saw them dozing.

"Thank God!" he sighed, checking to make sure I was okay. Sensing my angst, he reached back and squeezed my knee.

"It'll be okay, Liv," he reassured me.

To lighten the mood, he turned the radio on low, as the popular Captain & Tennille song, *Love Will Keep Us Together,* wafted gently through the air.

We both rubbed our eyes, and I shook my head to stay awake. Already 10 p.m., it seemed like the day would never end. I swallowed hard, wishing things would go back to normal.

We married young, just 10 months earlier. I was 19 and Sam was 20. Sam had enlisted in the Navy a year before, but both of us were wide-eyed and ready for adventure. Growing up in our Midwest, white-bred neighborhoods, you didn't lock your doors and kids came in from play when the streetlights came on. Diversity for us was Catholics and Lutherans in the same room with maybe the occasional Methodist or Episcopalian thrown in. When kids graduated from high school, they either went on to college, or tried to get a job at one of the many paper mills in the area. It was a mostly safe, but somewhat predictable existence. With Sam being in the military, that wasn't an option for us. And who wanted that anyway?

Four days after our wedding, equipped with our hopes and a huge paper map of the U.S., we packed up our belongings and drove to Sam's new duty station, Patuxent River Naval Air Test Center in Maryland. Just after crossing the state border from West Virginia into Maryland, we heard a siren and saw the red lights of a patrol car behind us. I couldn't believe it. Like it wasn't enough to have to drive across the country, now we were going to get a ticket too? I felt both nervous and angry. Sam pulled over and waited for the cruiser to pull up behind us. My heart thumped, and I saw tiny beads of sweat on Sam's forehead.

Striding leisurely toward the driver's side of the car, the officer motioned for Sam to roll down his window.

"Good afternoon, sir," he stated authoritatively while leaning on the side of the car. "Do y'all have any idea why I pulled you over?"

Of course, Sam knew. He was going 78 in a 65-mile per hour speed zone. *Why did troopers ask that kind of question?*

"Because I was speeding?" Sam asked tentatively.

"Yes, sir," the sheriff replied. Then he quoted the exact number of miles we'd been going over the limit and asked us where we were headed.

"I'm in the Navy and we are on our way to Patuxent River," Sam explained. He cleared his throat and continued sheepishly, "It's my first billet."

The officer paused and scratched his head as the stern look in his eyes tempered.

"Son," said the grizzled patrolman, tipping his hat back, "If that's the case, then you're going the wrong way."

He looked over and saw me wrestling with the map, frantically tracing our route across the paper with my finger.

"There's a Patuxent River in Maryland, but I believe y'all are looking for the naval air station, right?"

Yes, sir." Sam replied dutifully.

After explaining the new route, the officer let us off with a warning and a wish for good luck. We followed his directions all the way to the naval air station.

We arrived to find that the Navy had more personnel than they could house, so we moved into an old, World War II-era cinder block duplex just outside the base. Many of the military families found themselves in the same boat (so to speak), so we all lived in the same worn-out housing complex.

A small, rickety sidewalk leading from the road split and connected our house with our neighbors' place, where Lacey and Charles lived with their daughters, Dara and Deena. Though we looked nothing alike, Lacey and I were kindred spirits. We quickly became friends—me with my milky-white complexion and long, straight hair parted in the middle, and she, with her glossy, sable skin and a pick strategically placed in her whorled afro. She smiled with her whole face, her gap-toothed grin warm and inviting. We were both just poor enlisted wives trying to survive living in the same dumpy housing. We both shopped at the same low-end grocery store where bread was five loaves for a dollar, but I never suspected that it was considered a colored store.

Being educated in a middle-class white high school did nothing to prepare me for the reality of living in the South in 1975. My first glimpse of how things worked there was during a visit to the neighborhood laundromat. I'd set my basket of dirty laundry on the nearest washing machine and looked up to see a tall, African American man, clad in jeans and a black T-shirt with rolled up sleeves, his arms covered in tattoos. He stared at me as if in disbelief.

"Hello," I greeted him in my usual friendly, midwestern manner, trying to ignore his rudeness.

"What you doin' here?" he responded sharply, his eyes darting to the door and looking out the windows.

"My laundry," I replied, taken aback, and unnerved by his vaguely threatening response.

Recognizing my innocent foible in trespassing on a Black establishment, he scanned the room again, his response less harsh, his eyes speaking his concern.

"You need to leave right now," he instructed firmly. "White folks don't come to this place," he reiterated.

Seeing the dumbfounded look on my face, he scanned outside the windows again and continued, emphasizing every word, "You. Ain't. Safe.

Here. You understand?"

"Uh, okay," I said shakily, looking around as I finally realized the danger I was in. I quickly scooped up my basket and hastened out the door down the street to my house. My heart was pounding when I stepped onto my porch, turned the key, and slammed and locked the door. Then I dropped the basket and crumpled to the floor in tears.

When sharing my experience with Lacey later that day, she looked at me in astonishment.

"Girl, white folks don't go to that place! You a fool? You lucky you still breathing!" Then she gave me the address of the Wash-It across town. While it cost more to do my wash there, I became a regular.

As an E-2, Sam's salary was just one up from the lowest pay grade in the Navy, which put us well below the poverty level. I got a job in town at the dime store where they used cash registers from the early 1900s. Still, we struggled financially, and most of the time our diets consisted of ramen noodles, boxed macaroni and cheese, and, occasionally, baked chicken. Lacey and Charles didn't have much either, but she worked at the local Hardees and many times would bring home a few extra burgers for us. Sometimes that made a difference as to whether we ate that day. In return, I watched Lacey's kids so she could go to work. We were truly like sisters—at each other's houses often, and if our husbands weren't home, we'd just holler instead of knocking before entering.

The guys were in different squadrons and worked opposite shifts, so they never really got to know one another. Besides, Charles was generally cantankerous, and usually greeted us with a scowl. Oddly, he seemed popular enough, with a steady stream of people going in and out of the house when he was there.

It never occurred to me that Charles was dealing drugs until the day when a military police officer knocked on our door.

"Good afternoon, ma'am," the officer stated calmly as I opened it.

"Your neighbors are being arrested for drug possession, and the lady would like you to take the children."

Glancing past the officer, I saw Lacey being escorted out of her house in handcuffs, Charles a few steps ahead of her.

"Take the kids," she shouted at me as the MPs pushed her towards the car.

"And call Marie to come and get us," she cried, looking back at me. "They have her number," she yelled, nodding towards the cop.

Marie, Lacey's mother, lived in Michigan.

I was stunned. Sam was home and walked up behind me. I stepped out of the door, and another officer approached me with Dara and Deena in tow, both crying hysterically.

"Of course, we'll take them," I stuttered as he handed me baby Deena with a bottle in her mouth. Dara gripped her blanket with one hand, and wrapped her chubby arms around my leg with the other as her tears and snot mingled and flowed past her chin. I cuddled the children, holding them close as I tried not to cry. Then I gasped in pain as the baby in my belly kicked sharply.

I'd gotten pregnant almost on a whim, a couple of months after we were married. I was lonely living 1,800 miles away from my family, so why not start our own family? We agreed that we'd try and get pregnant. It worked almost immediately. Now seven months along, I never dreamed I'd be in a situation like this.

With a look of concern, Sam drew me close, putting his hand on my shoulder and gently guiding us all back into the house. In shock, with my heart pounding, I walked over to the wall phone and nervously dialed Marie's number.

"What have they gotten into now?" Marie asked in frustration when she answered the phone. After I explained the situation, she continued.

"Thank you for taking the girls," she said with a catch in her voice. "I'm so glad you were there."

The two-hour ride to the airport seemed to take forever. Sam and I walked nervously into the concourse, with Dara toddling between the two of us, and Deena on my right hip, sucking intently on her Nuk and resting her tiny hand on my obviously pregnant girth.

"Oh my!" I heard one lady exclaim as she walked past us, shaking her head. I looked around to see what she was talking about.

A couple approaching us looked me up and down before grunting in disgust and turning around. I swallowed hard and tried to gaff it off.

"They're talking about us!" I whispered to Sam, nudging him as Deena snuggled onto my shoulder.

People sitting on the benches lining both sides of the aisle lowered their newspapers to see what the fuss was about. Some just stared and dropped their jaws, while others shook their heads and raised their papers again to block their views.

One man boldly stepped forward, and with hatred in his eyes, pointed his finger at us and shouted, "Go home! You don't belong here!"

I felt embarrassed and hurt.

What's the big deal? I reasoned with myself, trying to ignore the blatant bigotry we were experiencing. *We're just two folks from Wisconsin helping some friends from Michigan.*

But to these people, it mattered. In fact, to them, we were quite a spectacle. They saw a poor, young, white couple with two small black children. And me, big and pregnant. In their eyes, I was white trash, an interracial tramp! I wanted to laugh and cry at the same time. Was this what it felt like to be on the other side of the white/Black fence? I was filled with shame and confusion. For what it looked like, for how I felt, and for how we were treated. And what about the two children who were with us? Would they have to face this sort of prejudice their entire lives? It was infuriating.

I'd only felt a fraction of what Lacey and other people of color must feel all the time. I thought about the colored grocery store, the colored laundromat, and the many other colored establishments I'd seen, and the hands of racism and segregation slapped me hard in the face. I finally realized that no matter how nicely it was packaged, this world treated certain people poorly, despite what was taught in schools or preached from the pulpit. My idealistic, kumbaya world was shattered, and I would never see the world in the same way again.

Sam clasped my hand and our eyes met in unspoken agreement regarding the safety and care of the tender souls entrusted to us. We put our heads down and beelined it to the gate where we welcomed Marie with open arms.

The kids woke up long enough to greet their grandma with a few tears and the cry of "Nana!" before nodding off again. After quick hugs and some small talk, we all walked back through the airport together with our heads held high, leaving our rose-colored glasses behind, and venturing into what was for us, a new frontier.

As for Charles, the Navy took him into custody, summoned him to a Captain's Mast–a form of military justice–and was dishonorably discharged. The State of Maryland then arrested him for possession with intent to sell, and he ended up serving jail time.

Marie bailed Lacey out of jail the next day, and Lacey stopped by afterward to thank me. We chatted for a while, and out of curiosity I asked her why she called her mother Marie instead of mom. Turns out she and Marie had grown apart years ago when Lacey decided to marry Charles. Marie told her that Charles was no good and refused to come to their wedding. Lacey figured no decent mother would do such a thing and started calling her Marie instead of mom after that.

In the end, Marie was right about Charles. Lacey left him, and now that she and Marie were on good terms, she and the girls moved back to Michigan with her mom. Of course, we stayed in touch.

Sam and I moved on base that month, so we got a break on our rent. We still struggled to make ends meet though. For Christmas that year, we got each other a $7 bottle of Avon cologne, and spent $15 for a used bassinet. Things were bleak.

Then, out of nowhere, five days before Christmas, we received a huge package in the mail. The return address was Marie's. I opened it to find a complete layette for the baby, including blankets, diapers, clothing, and a sweet little teddy bear.

At the bottom of the box was a card that included a $100 check for us and a note that read: "Thank you for caring for my girls when I couldn't. You will both be in our hearts forever. God bless you and your little family, and know that you are welcome in my home anytime."

The next summer, Sam, little Sam, and I took a trip to Michigan.

Kodiak Island

Ryan Surprise

After another day of patrolling their sleepy little town, the Kodiak Island Police Department had received instructions to search the premises of a cabin on the outskirts of the small fishing village. Jack Murray's next of kin had made the call to search his home. A few miles deep into the woods stood the peeling, second-hand, cottage where Jack Murray had spent most of his nights.

After the police cruiser had silenced its engine, the stillness of the night air encapsulated the surroundings. The peaceful silence suddenly exploded with a blow to the front door. The two deputies lowered the battering ram with a thud on the porch. They squeezed through the gap in the doorway and searched the home. A woman wrapped in a fashionable winter coat stepped in after them.

"Any place we should look first?" one of the deputies asked her.

"His room, I guess," she suggested.

Flashlights scanned over the surfaces of the living room. Balls of dust laid their claim in the corners of the cabin. Wrinkled flannels and a dirty plate sat on the arm of the couch. Unlucky lottery numbers and $5 chips from a Seattle casino sprawled out across the kitchen table.

Inside the bedroom, the first deputy locked eyes on the nightstand. He took it upon himself to secure the left-behind revolver and emptied its contents. One .38 caliber bullet thumped against the pillow at a time.

Still standing in the living room, the woman's eyes wandered around the mess before resting on a large revolving chalkboard covering the wall. Numbers crowded the board with acronyms accompanying the largest numbers, like MPH, Hrs, and Gal. She pushed the bottom of the board to tip it closer to her outstretched hand. On the reverse side of the board was a map of the southern Alaskan islands. Three strands of string trailed from a large green pin on Kodiak Island. She looked closer at the strings' destination but it was open sea.

"Is this the safe, Natalie?" one of the deputies asked her. She pulled herself from the chalkboard.

"Yes," she muttered. The first deputy set the revolver down and tried the combination: Jack's birthday. The number pad flashed, and the numbers on the screen disappeared.

"One, nineteen, seventy-three, right?" he asked.

"That's the one," she said. He tried again. The second deputy flashed his light around the nightstand, looking for clues. The numbers disappeared again.

"Anything else?" he asked.

"September first, ninety-nine," she suggested. He pressed the nine, then the one, and then nine-nine. The screen shined bright and the bolt inside retracted.

"There we go," he said, opening the safe. Documents, the deed to the house, and a wad of a few thousand dollars sat inside.

"What date was that?" The deputy asked.

"It used to be our anniversary," she muttered.

Jack Murray's old SUV wrenched forward, rolling back on a six-inch snow bank of its own making. Jack reached over into the back seat. A heavy duffle bag sagged as he tried to thread it through the gap between the two front seats. Cursing his way through it, it flopped into his lap.

Stepping out of the vehicle, he slipped the sling over his shoulder. His boots crunched the fresh snow underfoot, bringing him closer to the plowed airstrip. Inside the hangar was the manager/clerk/security guard, Morris. His right hand loosely held a mug in place, while the other held his head up as he caught up on his sleep. The frigid cold nipped at his nose, with a wet drip clinging to his nostril precariously over his morning coffee.

Morris heard a tapping and groaned at his misfortune to be needed. Jack's fist still tapped against the glass of his four-foot by four-foot office. Morris met him at the window.

"I'm taking the plane out," Jack said.

"Alright, do you need gas?" Morris slurred.

"I filled it up last time," Jack reassured him. He threw Morris a two-finger salute before sauntering off to the little Piper Cub sitting in the cold. Jack climbed up the side of the machine and threw the door open. The cabin could just fit three small people inside it. His duffle bag took up the back bench seats. The single-pilot vessel sputtered and eased out of the hangar.

Jack gave it some gas as soon as he turned the plane onto the airstrip. Everything shook as the plane accelerated. Jack's sunglasses used the bridge of his nose like a trampoline. Gaining more speed, Jack readied himself for takeoff. He pulled up on the yoke. His stomach felt a funny little lift. Soaring through the air and adjusting his ailerons. Jack's lip curled as he saw the icy sea water beneath him.

On his joy rides, Jack liked to look for the best view of the Alaskan coastline. He imagined how some city slickers might never want to leave Seattle or Denver but, for him, the wilderness with its untouched natural beauty always satisfied. With the fresh snowfall the night before, the gray clouds laid low. Just low enough for a single-engine joy flier to touch.

Before ascending further above the crashing waves, Jack reached into his pocket and looked at a folded map. His finger traced his path from the white splotch labeled Kodiak Island. Running his fingernail westward along the map, another white splotch, like a mustard seed, met his nail. He leaned over to the window and saw the little rock bracing itself against the waves. He examined his wristwatch.

"Twenty minutes," he muttered. He dragged his nail further west, passing other small islands, before reaching a drawn circle in the middle of the ocean. He measured the distance he made in 20 minutes and estimated he would arrive in nearly an hour. He set the map aside and reached back into his duffle bag. His brow furrowed, wondering what he was missing.

"Where'd you go?" Jack muttered. He tapped his fingers around the bag and retrieved a heavy camera with a large lens. He set it next to him on the bench seat before manhandling the yoke to take him to the clouds.

The features beneath him shrank in scope, and his altitude reader swung up and up. Another deep breath comforted him as the air thinned around the plane. The plane pierced the clouds, leaving the blue beneath him in a foggy haze. Soon Jack could only see the deep fathoms of the clouds through his windscreen. He bit his lip, pulling on the yoke as far as it could go. He would never admit he was afraid but he certainly didn't like to fly blind for long. Finally, the wisps of the cloud appeared ahead of him and his little flying machine burst through to see the vast, brilliant ecosystem of blue skies above a gray cloud bottom.

Despite sitting in a metal box at 7,000 feet in the air, the sunlight warmed Jack in his cabin. He pressed the switch labeled *Autopilot* and sighed a victorious groan as he spread his back against his seat.

Jack swept his eyes over the beautiful view. The open ocean came closer, blending in with the blue horizon. Jack's eyes sagged. The exterior warmth made him feel comfortable and he leaned his head back, crossing his arms until they sank into his lap, waiting to reach the islands.

Jack sucked in air through his nose at the sound of radio chatter. He listened again, hearing nothing. He examined his readings, still holding steady at 7,000 feet. He looked at his fuel tank, only half empty. He had plenty of fuel to get back or make a skip-and-a-hop back to Kodiak Island. He read his watch. He had been cruising for an hour now.

He looked down below, finding blue, frigid waters around him on all sides. He disengaged the autopilot and dipped the plane down to get a better look. As he descended, his squinting brow shot up.

"There you are," he said with a tooth-licking grin. Through the windscreen he could see the plain, treeless island that he had been looking for. Covered in snow and large rock formations, Jack was shocked the first time he saw it as it was nowhere to be found on the map. As he pushed down on the yoke, he lifted the heavy camera to his windscreen. The sun glared through the glass, but he had to take as many photographs as he could. In the camera's viewfinder, Jack saw the crisp image of the island thousands of feet beneath him.

Soon, the Piper Cub passed the island. Jack turned his camera to the side window and carefully adjusted the controls to turn while keeping the island within the center of his lens.

"November Two-Niner, identify yourself, over." A voice came through the radio. Jack reached for the radio, thinking what to say.

"This is Geoff Goldstein, November Two-Niner, just passing through, over."

"Turn around and go home. You are trespassing, over."

Jack kept turning around the island, squinting at the word "trespassing". He had never heard of such a thing since he had learned how to fly. He took more pictures of the island, looking away from the viewfinder to see the whole island.

"This is November Two-Niner, who am I speaking with?" Jack asked the radio. There was no response.

"Is there a radio station on this island?" he asked into the radio. Jack set his camera aside and maneuvered to swing a wide loop around the island while descending closer.

"This is your final warning," the voice beckoned.

Jack clasped the radio harder and lied through his teeth. "This is November Two-Niner, I am a cartographer for the Alaskan Survey."

A thunderous boom swept past him. His hand clasped the back of his head. A thick vein began to throb against his palm. *What was that?* Suddenly, the plane tipped down and Jack saw his plane nosedive towards earth. Every arrow on the altitude reader began swinging wildly downward.

"Woah! Woah!" Jack hollered as he took hold of the yoke. He pulled as hard as he could. His hands started to sweat as he felt the machine's indifference to his demand of the controls. He pushed it in and yanked it out to only find loose unresponsiveness.

"Come on!" He gave it a smack. He noticed the light above *Autopilot* was still on. He flipped it and jerked back with the controls. He lunged forward with a new sense of fatigue. His eyes ran to the altitude reader. He had fallen 2,500 feet and gaining with the engine driving him downward. His goose was cooked. He wrenched the radio handset to his chin and opened the airwaves.

"Mayday! Mayday! Mayday! November Two-Niner, control malfunction! Anybody, come in, over!"

Jack turned off the engine. Letting gravity do the work would give him a few more vital seconds. He pulled on the yoke back and forth, left and to the right, but nothing. He was crashing at 55 meters per second and had just descended below 2,500 feet. He figured he had less than a minute to pull himself out of this mess. His remaining options weren't promising.

"Jack Murray of November Two-Niner, fifty-plus miles west of Kodiak Island," he sighed, preparing himself for the raging waters climbing toward him. *This is going to hurt.*

"Come on!" He screamed, screamed to stop the thoughts in his head. Screamed to wake up the controls. At the top of his lungs, he felt the ailerons snap down. The resistance in the yoke came back, and he slammed his feet into the wall to brace himself. The machine buckled up and up, getting more and more level with the turbulent waters. His engine was still off but he knew a safer landing would need less speed, especially as the whitecaps looked like surfboards.

Jack figured he was only ten meters above sea level so all he had to do was lightly touch the water and break his speed. It was easier said than done but he licked his lips and tightened his grip on the controls.

His confidence sank when he saw a patch of white less than a mile ahead of him. An island, some rock in the middle of nowhere, and he couldn't go up or around it in time. He jutted the yoke up just to get a taste of the waves on his landing gear. One large wave clapped the side of the vessel and nearly turned him around. Jack gritted his teeth and balanced himself again. He tried it again but felt another uncontrollable kick in the side.

This is going to hurt. The rock caught up to him. The snow-covered boulders on the flanks of the island caught his wheels. A metallic screech came with the tearing of the landing gear, nearly tipping the plane upside down. Jake controlled the machine until it smashed into a snow drift.

The crash thrust Jack into the yoke and cut his knee like an axe. Jack saw white and foamed at the mouth from the horrific pain. The spit in the back of his throat choked him as he cried out.

The windscreen was entirely covered in snow, with no light coming through. Jack jiggled the door. He needed more force to push it free. He looked down at his cut knee and tried to keep it steady as he pushed with his good leg. Enough of a gap for him to slide through became available. His injured leg started to tighten, and he watched it carefully as he reached behind him for a better grip outside of the plane. His back strained, his arms ached at every pull, but he knew he could get out. Once his back hit the soft snow, he pressed his tongue between his teeth and gave it another go.

Once his wounded leg came through the threshold, he looked around. The cold started to bite under his coat. He saw some figures in the distance. He must have landed somewhere populated. Some men started to run. *They weren't too far off*, Jack told himself. Only…it was strange. The closer they got, the more seemed to appear. They all came running. Was no one going for help or to call an ambulance?

Then their coats became clearer; they were brown, working coats. That wasn't uncommon, of course, but they were all wearing them, the same khaki brown. Their boots kept pounding snow. Jack watched them close in. They'd have answers for him, but there were dozens of them, all in the same brown coats. As soon as he could see the whites of their eyes, the helpful, shocked expressions he had hoped to see were absent. The men wore furrowed brows and bared their teeth.

"Wait! Stop!" he shouted to them. "Wait!"

"Good evening, you're listening to Declassified News," a gravelly voice said to a microphone. "We have a report of a plane going missing off the coast of Alaska… I know what you're thinking, who cares about a small plane that went missing? Jack Murray wasn't a government agent and wasn't a threat to national security, but he saw something that he wasn't supposed to see. We have someone who has valuable information on this case right now, Natalie."

"Hi, Rick," Natalie said, a little nervous to hear herself on air considering the grave subject. "Jack Murray was my…my first husband. We lived on Kodiak Island. When Jack went missing, I found information on where he was heading. He was a pleasure pilot and had marked his flight pattern, where I came across something that I still can't quite believe.

"The facts are that Jack flew out around nine a.m. the day he disappeared. His plane, a Piper Cub, has a range of about 150 miles. According to the radio transmission he sent off before going missing, he was somewhere between fifty to a hundred miles west of Kodiak. A personal friend flew me out on that same path to look for his plane. I thought maybe we could find some surviving wreckage, but as soon as I hit the fifty-mile mark, you'll never believe this, I got a warning on the radio."

"What kind of warning, Natalie?"

"Two fighter jets came along either side of me and told me to turn around, I had breached military airspace."

"Were you anywhere near an army base?"

"No, this was the middle of the ocean. The nearest coastline was maybe twenty miles from us, but these two jets cornered us, and we radioed back to tell them we didn't want any trouble, and we turned back around, but I kept an eye out behind us and they followed us for a while, so…"

"So just by flying the same direction that Jack Murray had, you had breached military airspace, someplace the government doesn't want you to be?"

"That's right, and before I turned around, I saw an island, someplace that's not on the map. In my ex-husband's home, I found a map of his that tracked his flight pattern before. In this area where we had flown by, he had it circled on his map. On the map at his home and on new maps that I cross-referenced, I could find no markings of any island in that vicinity."

"Could you tell what was on the island, any military fortifications?"

"No," Natalie said, somewhat taken aback. "There wasn't anything like that, but I've done some digging on possible clues. On the night Jack went missing, a ship saw a fire in that direction. They called in to see if it was another ship, but they got no response, and the fire didn't go down, they said, so it wasn't a sinking ship."

"It was the island."

"I think Jack crash landed on the island. If the fire started after he crashed, it wouldn't have been visible late at night. I think something happened on the island. Someone set his plane on fire to destroy evidence of him being there."

"Why would someone do that, do you think?"

"Those planes that fly over that island carry cargo, and it's not a military base, I know that, but when you're dropping supplies to an island that's not on the map, you don't want folks to know who's there or why."

"Political prisoners?"

"It's possible… some place they haven't told us about."

"So who did him in, the government or the prisoners?"

Natalie balked at the question. In all her searching, she somehow imagined that Jack could still be alive. That maybe he could still be found. Maybe he was locked away on that island.

"They might have thought Jack was one of the cargo plane pilots," she offered. "Keeping them on the island but only giving them enough tools to survive, or… I don't know. Maybe I'm out of–"

"Thanks, Natalie, after a word from our sponsor, we'll have an exclusive report on UFO sightings and what exactly the government knows about extraterrestrials here on earth."

The Third Son and the Fourth Caesar

Max DeMay

AD 69

A lot of hay can be made over why I went. These woods are so far from what anyone knows. I can't put my finger on it. I couldn't stay one more day in Rome.

My father warned me there would be no comforts, no food. I wish he were right. In the legion, I looked for a life that was simpler, harder. Instead, there's more food here than I've ever known. Drink too. When we make camp, our bonfires pile high above the peat bogs. The men are loud these nights. The only difference to Rome is when they whoop and shout, there's no one to call back.

Ever since Vitellius was made our general it's been like this. More wine has flowed than blood. He came all of a sudden and from far away. Before, I was quietly making a name, going up in rank, but he brought his own guys. I'm not in their circle. With us, his men are loud and smiling, but when they turn to each other, they speak in low whispers.

Before we crossed into Germania, the world's end, a land of trees and mossy men, weird women, we stopped outside a tower I didn't like the looks of. Like the rest of the country, the tower was dark and wet. It bent like a beggar to the border river. A wall of dead logs circled it. All the land for a mile had been axed.

The man of the tower was Gaius Commodus. As we neared his fort, he galloped out to meet us. He had only one eye. The other had been cut out.

Vitellius, on a grand steed, met the ragged figure halfway. At a distance from us, he parlayed with this Gaius Commodus, making a show of it. Vitellius was a big man and moved big when he talked. His skin was burnt, browner than mine, charred by the sunfire out of Africa. He was on the far side of the sea for a long time, so they told.

After some words, Gauis and Vitellius seemed to hack a rough deal on the length and like of our stay. Without patience, I waited for the report to come back to us. He brought it to his officers first.

Finally, they brought it to us. We would cross the river in three days. First, though, they needed a man to volunteer himself for an important task. Most shuffled and found their feet.

"Tertius Suetonius," I called.

That's my name—Tertius. It's not much. I'm the third son of a father who thought there would be two others to carry his name.

As I stepped up, Vitellius handed me a clinking bag. I took it. Heavy as it was, it held, with no doubt, a hefty mass of gold. I thought I'd never see such an unholy sum again. Nothing in these woods was worth it.

"Gaius promises much," Vitellius said. "Follow him. If he has the goods, the pay is due."

What Gaius promised, I didn't dare ask.

Not wanting to be alone in my strange errand, I took with me a Gaul who marched by me for much of the road. All the way, he walked with a steady step, easy to match. His hair was black as a raven. His calf muscles were strong.

While the rest made camp, Gaius Commodus dismounted and led me, his horse, and the Gaul to his tower. I did not think the tower sound but did not fail in my step. Vitellius watched from his steed with a set, heavy gaze. The door to Gauis' fort opened a peek and, once we were in, clacked shut.

Eyes dogged us across the yard. Gaius Commodus had a little band under him. What I saw of the shifty figures did not look like soldiers. I put their number at a little over the fingers on two hands, not enough to hold their little part of the border from invaders.

Entering the tower, Gaius led us down. My belt sagged under the gold's weight. Narrow as the passage was, we went down single file, the Gaul in back. Torches, stabbed into the stone, shone the way. Their fumes caused the air to hum.

Gaius talked all the way down.

"Might it be you find our accommodations lacking," Gaius said. "We've not had the likes of you and your host for a while! Let us prove! Make no mistake—we love all our guests. You'll not excuse the hospitality.

"We've little to do but entertain," Gaius went on. "Not a peep from across the river. Strange, you think, but it's true. Been years since a good fight."

"Maybe the Germanians know they're licked," the Gaul said.

I glimpsed up and behind. The Gaul had not seemed one for talk. We shared no words the entire long march. Gaius crooked his head, also taken aback that the pale Gaul had been the one to speak and not I.

"But we've not licked them!" Gaius exclaimed.

"They just know."

Over my shoulder, I shot a look at the Gaul to silence him. If he said something foolish, it would be me to pay. I did not think he got my meaning.

Gaius shrugged. He seemed to be not a curious man. The stairs stopped at the entrance to a chamber of stone. To go on, we had to duck under an opening in the rock. The rock was marked by many letters. I can read a few words, but picked out none. Whatever it said, it stopped the Gaul dead.

"I know these."

Gaius halted, forcing me to stop. His torch flew into my face. I had to look away.

"They're not ours," Gaius said.

"No, they are not," the Gaul said. "They are much older."

Gaius tapped his foot.

"Mayhaps, Julius Caesar's?"

"Even before."

"From when then, mister?"

"I don't know."

Gaius threw up his free hand.

"I know they're an omen of no good thing," the Gaul said.

"What thou doesn't know can't hurt thee!" Gaius exclaimed.

"We should not be here."

Gaius's nose scrunched. His teeth clenched, a wolfish display even through the gaps. I was party to every twist in shape. I'm not one for omens, but the Gaul's words did chill me. In any way, the warning did me no good— I was already through the door.

"This is a bad deal," the Gaul stated.

He addressed these words to me, wanting my answer. It was too much. He dared question Vitellius' orders. The way he went on, it was as if I were not in charge.

"We've got orders!" I exclaimed.

"We have no business here," the Gaul said.

I'd never heard such fear in a man's voice. The tone of it echoed in the small space hitting me like a long flurry of punches. I had to fight back. Small thinking was what it was. The more the Gaul stuck me with his eyes, the angrier I got.

"Enough!" I shouted. "It's in your head!"

Mutely, the Gaul's eyes widened. Though we'd shared no words on the march, I thought we understood each other. We were soldiers, bound to show no fear. Weird runes or no, the Gaul slunk through the threshold with the rest of us. Gaius rolled his eyes.

We entered the cave. The dark chamber looked so familiar, I thought I was many years ago and far away in my father's olive oil shop—a store full of tall clay vessels that, as a kid, I couldn't move without risk of knocking over. The cave held more clay vessels than ten of my father's shops. I did not think they held anything as simple as oil. They were placed on rough shelves, three-stacked. At spots, shelves were done away with and there were only clay vessels, one on one, in piles. The torch did not go far enough. The chamber stretched beyond seeing. Hints of other chambers showed themselves left and right, wound and winding.

If it weren't for the crackle of Gaius's torch, no sound came.

"What's in these?" I asked.

"What was promised," Gaius said.

Picking a vessel at random, I sniffed what it held. Right away, the sharp smell threw me back. The red of it was darker than blood.

"These are all full of wine?" I asked.

In the ill-light, I caught Gaius's grin.

"Not all."

From down the cavern, as if Gaius told a joke, came a woman's laugh. I stiffened. I faced the darkness. No one was there, but there were many places one could hide. I palmed the heel of my sheathed sword. Laughter echoed no more. When I shot a look at Gaius, he gave no sign that he had heard another. His hand floated up and out, in waiting.

I turned to the Gaul. He was no help, blank, staring at a wall. I'd been alone in hearing the laugh.

A few shadows and a laugh—Vitellius would not hear such an excuse. All I had to do was tell if the value of the wine was worth the gold. I wanted the heavy sack off my belt. I handed Gaius the bag.

Unstringing his prize, Gaius emptied a coin into his hand. He peered through it with his only eye. They were fresh coins, glimmery, wearing the hawk-face of our new emperor. He gnawed on one. In that icky perch, between Gaius's teeth, the emperor did not change his sneer. Gaius nodded.

"The deal is made," Gaius said.

All this time, the Gaul stayed silent. A strange concern for this outsider came over me, which made gentle the words I meant to be harsh.

"What is it?"

The Gaul did not hear. His eyes were like marbles.

"What do you see?"

Coming out of his dream, the Gaul turned to me. He did not answer in words. Instead, he pointed.

Plastered on the cave wall, from behind a clay vessel, kicked a big black hoof. What monster it belonged to, I could not guess for it was not a leg by itself. At once, the Gaul and I attacked the shelves, tearing away the heavy vessels.

Our violent clatter did not dint our host. Gaius stood at the threshold with his gold, nibbling one after one, feasting like he was at a festival. Both hands were used in this task. He'd disarmed his torch, placing it into a hole in the wall. There, the flame flailed, growing small.

When the wall was bare, I saw what made the Gaul freeze up—animals of all ilk painted onto the stone. I saw the head of one and the haunch of another. Among the monsters, the largest was a black ox. The black hoof I'd seen was from the leg of that big ox. Many men, sticks by comparison, holding thin spears, hunted the beast. Such a noble monster I'd never seen, though I'd heard tales.

Egging them on were women, woven through the cave of charcoal, ash, and blood. Their forms, never more than crude, cast a net. They danced around the hunt. Carved around them were more runes like those that halted the Gaul. Past where the light could touch, the scene went on. What we saw was only a sliver.

"These are older than the trees," the Gaul said.

Against the wall, the torch flickered and died. The cave disappeared into darkness.

Older than the trees.

Three days passed from when the Gaul put these words in me and I couldn't get them out. I meant to ask the Gaul the age of trees, but it was a tough thing to ask. When we made eye contact, it was strained. We both saw things we shouldn't've. As a company, we crossed the river burdened with wine, and left Gaius and his cave far behind. I couldn't get away fast enough.

There's one comfort in our camp I've not told of, and that is the comfort of women. I don't know how they got here. They showed up, one by one, with silent steps, from behind the trees. Vitellius's officers say they are Germanic women of the Chatti tribe. I've not heard of Germanic women in so many shades of skin. They were all sizes, large and small, tall and short. They dressed strange, wearing robes of many colors. Others, in the cold, wore almost nothing. Even the oldest among them looked young. One woman, a seeress she said, claimed to have seen more winters than any of us, but looked to have lived through twenty. While the other women were free to all, she held counsel only with Vitellius. They closed themselves off in his grand tent.

Though these women were as plentiful as the wine and food, they were jostled over. Men had their favorites. They wasted much time fighting for the attention of their loves. The crimes of the city followed us. These Chattian women were trouble. I knew this straight away and made no use of them.

One night, our seventh behind the river, the men were only starting to drink and the sun was only starting to set, its last red arms reaching without sound across the marsh, when I heard shouting. Some eleven of us heard. It came from Vitellius's tent. We rushed over.

Always glomming to him, Vitellius' many smiling officers were somewhere gone. From its flaps, a woman had been thrown outside into the mud. Her purple robes were ruined. Vitellius stood over her, eyes popping out of his head.

"You lie!" Vitellius shouted.

It was the seeress in the mud. Though her voice held, she seemed in no good way.

"It is already done," the seeress said. "When your mother dies—you will inherit all of Rome."

Where no wrinkles scarred her, there were wrinkles now. Her youth was taking off with the sun. Seeing her changed sent shivers down me. I don't go for magic, but some evil trick was at play. Arms flayed, Vitellius spoke to the sky.

"A cursed prophecy you make! A burden you put on me! I love my mother! Why would I want such a thing!? A witch! All of you! Witches!"

Vitellius gazed up. His finger jabbed. He was pointing at me.

"You, man!" Vitellius shouted. "Expel these witches from my camp! I want them gone before the sun!"

Given such an errand, from our leader himself, I sprung to it. It should've been done long ago. Of the eleven around, I took charge. Starting with the seeress, we rounded up the women, casting them back to the woods. So well and fast we did our work, we did not even allow time for many to grab their clothes. They were sent bare into the wild.

Some tried to stop us. A large man from Pompeii named Charis, stood between me and his favorite, a dusky beauty. Driven by duty, I was forced into fisticuffs. Swords were drawn.

I got into a lot of fights in Rome. I'm not proud of it. My father called me an urchin. Swords, large and awkward, were never used. Daggers were more our speed.

Careless, I nicked Charis' arm. Blood splashed onto my tunic, drying right away. Charis stopped fighting. I took the woman away. It was no great feat—the man was drunk. The first battle I had in Germania was one I might have had in Rome.

As Vitellius commanded, the women were out before dark. My duty was done. The men, though, were restless. They muttered, mumbled, and cursed. They had been ready to settle into an easy night. Dodging scowls, I made my report back at the tent.

"This will not be forgotten," Vitellius said. "You have done well, Tertius."

Vitellius' mighty neck nodded. A single grand gesture and I was raised into the ranks of his graces. With his eyebrows, he bade me come closer. For the first time, I heard him speak in a whisper, but a loud whisper. Had there been an audience, they'd all have heard.

"And down in the cave too…" Vitellius began. "…that was a delicate moment. Your discretion is noted."

It jarred me that Vitellius mentioned the cave at all. Sometimes, times that have passed are better thought of as dreams, or things that didn't happen at all. That's what I did with my thoughts of Rome. It's what I try to do with the cave.

"It is well, but for one thing…"

I stiffened, knowing what it was.

"You took a man down there with you," Vitellius said. "A foreigner. A Gaul, I think. Can you vouch for this man?"

I kept my gaze low, but did not fail to notice the short sword he held. It was a display piece, but plenty sharp. I'm a man to give answers straight and true. Lying is the vice of Rome, of all its business-keeps and senators. The Gaul did not like the cave. He did not like the deal. At the wrong times, he was a talker.

"Trust him," I said. "Like I hope you trust me."

After some weighing and thinking, Vitellius put down his display piece. I shouldn't have lied, but the Gaul was a different beast. He had a strange honor. Strange honor was the best I'd found so far. Vitellius no longer minded me. He turned his mind to other things.

"There appears to be a great commotion," Vitellius said.

Driven by a rogue goat-skin drum, the men were making their anger known. Not a small number were surrounding his tent. Many thought they'd been wronged of something that was theirs.

It is a great fortune to Vitellius his grinning officers appeared about this time. They came weighted with gifts. Vitellius opened his own store of goods and threw a feast. Never have I seen such as was served. More trees were felled for the bonfire. So great did the blaze grow that it sucked wet from the marsh until it no longer felt like winter. Lambs and goats were brought from the rear and killed on the spot, their meat blackened and served by the haunch.

Cheeses, wheels of them, were laid on logs, like a fungus. Oysters were thrown about as if by Neptune riding the waves, sweet and chilled and still alive.

Some drunken ass found a wild ox stuck and baying in the marsh. They slit its throat and threw it on the fire with the rest.

Throughout this food-drunk orgy, I sought the Gaul. We were tied up in danger, he had to be warned, but he was not an easy man to find. I cascaded through the party, but could not remain a ghost. Avoiding glares, I partook as the men partook. The wine tasted bitter. It bit back like blood on a broken lip. Even with the vile drink in my stomach, they would not let me be.

"Tertius," they called. "Banisher of Women, Prude of Germania!"

"Lay off," I said.

They should know I was with Vitellius, one of his own. I wasn't a nameless soldier. As they surrounded me, I looked for his officers, my new fellows. They were spread out in threes and fours, mired in important talk.

"Couldn't bear to see us get a little action, while he got none."

Two men grabbed me from behind. I twisted and turned, but there was no besting them. They raised me up, and I was on their shoulders upon a sea of drunk and over-full men.

At the foot of a large stump, they dumped me. One started beating again on that flayed goat-skin drum. *KA-dum, KA-dum, KA-dum.* Any words I could say to stop what they were doing were already gone, wasted.

Charis, the man of Pompeii, arm in a sling, stood behind me on the stump holding a large clay vessel. With great and wicked joy, he swished it back and forth, eager to pour what it held on my head.

"Tertius! Tertius! Tertius!" they chanted.

Years, many useless years, manning my father's shop, and I solved the riddle of what the vessel held without it needing to be poured. It was olive oil.

"Hail, Tertius Suetonius, Caesar of the Wild! Caesar of the Wastes! What need of women has he? What need of love?"

They'd never understand. All they wanted was vice. Greatness couldn't be gained that way. A man couldn't live like a sheep for all time. I grabbed what I could. They couldn't blame me for that.

Messengers from faraway saved me from my coming bath. Seven in sum, they broke into the camp on horseback. With a piercing shout, their cry rallied the men, hailing for Vitellius. Out of the shadows, into the realm of his men, he appeared dressed in his cleanest purple robes. All eyes locked on his great figure.

"I am here," Vitellius said.

"Your mother is dead."

A hush fell, the only quiet that whole night. Through hearsay, all the camp had heard the Chattian seeress' prophecy. Vitellius' face twisted into a mask of abject horror. He cried out the name of his mother. He withered and fell to his knees. We could only watch.

As Vitellius sobbed, the messenger read the letter in full. Vitellius' mother died in intense pain, a victim of hunger. The old woman's guts had twisted and torn until her women-in-waiting could feed her no more. Evil detail, I did not stick around to hear it all. It was time for me to be scarce. The cheer echoed as I reached the woods' edge. Our prophecy came true. We were among a true Caesar—God on Earth.

I took refuge in a trench dug outside the camp. Water seeped through its edges. Sitting in that trench, I might have even cried. I'd left everything to join the legion, marched miles to the world's edge. Rome followed me. It spited me still. Its evil could not be fled. I sat in its murderous stink.

In the dirt, the Gaul found me. Without words, he slid down beside me. He gripped my shoulder like a brother. His green eyes were glass. It made me mad to look at them.

"How old are trees?" I asked.

The Gaul blinked two and three times. There'd been something more important that I'd meant to tell him, but I could only see the trees.

"The riddle you gave me," I repeated. "What is older than the trees?"

Woebegone, the Gaul shook his head. He stared at the trench's other wall.

"Nothing is older than the trees. You might as well say older than the skies, older than the stars. All are older than we will ever know."

He answered in a way that would never make any sense. I thought and thought but my mind would not get it.

"They can only grow older," the Gaul concluded.

I remembered what I needed to tell him.

"We're in great danger," I said.

The Gaul's hand stilled on my shoulder. He didn't seem surprised, but I sensed fear growing, creeping.

"That cave…" the Gaul began.

"I shouldn't have given that man the gold," I said.

The Gaul shook his head.

"That was not a man," the Gaul said.

Gauis—I didn't believe in ghosts, but if any man were not a man it would be him.

"We need to stick together," I said.

"Promise?"

In the distance, the bonfire blew to new heights, a fireball, hailing a new Caesar. Using an old dagger, we made a pact in blood.

As a citizen of this empire, you'll know what happened next. We did indeed march on Rome. Vitellius gave me a new place towards the front. Fitting for my new rank, I kept a footman—the Gaul.

By accident, on our march, we bumped into another man who called himself Caesar. This pretender was not the hawk-faced geezer on so many of Vitellius' coins. That one had been beheaded by his own men while on holiday in Hispania.

This new false Caesar was not worth naming. He was a pushover. On the third night of pitched battle, he killed himself.

I woke that fourth morning, primed for blood. Instead, we ended up milling about. With nothing to do, we crossed the swamp and hailed our dead rival's men. Some of them went on to march with us.

Rome greeted Vitellius as a hero. The city had been waiting for a mighty military man. On his chestnut bay, our great commander struck the figure of a Caesar. That very day, ten thousand coins were minted of his long face and mighty neck.

Vitellius ruled Rome much like he ruled Germania. In the bowels of the Earth there must be many such caves as Gauis'. Each day, the streets reeked of wine. The Colosseum put on two shows a day until they ran out of great beasts, slaves, and hard men. To keep the games going, they staged fights between women.

I never had a taste for games. I spent my days riding through the city with the Gaul. Vitellius made me a deputy. I kept the law. In Rome, it always needed keeping. I worked as hard as I could cleaning up the wretched streets I'd ran through as a child, but the morning sun always rose on new piles of slop. I got to feeling at odds with Vitellius. I'd clear an alley of drunkards only for him to ship another galley full of wine into the city.

One day we stopped in at my father's shop. Some old instinct led me. It was good that I did. Three months prior, when I'd been away on tour, my father died. An old servant told me so. The shop was due to change hands. All my father got from the sale had been willed to me.

I once believed my father was done with me. He thought of me, I guess, on his final bed. Maybe he loved me. Maybe, like me, he had no one else.

The Gaul and I spent late nights arguing over what to do with the gold. I wanted to cast it into the sea. The Gaul was more cool-headed. There were ways to make a chunk of gold last until the end of one's days. Prudence bored me. Add up gold all you want, it will always slip through your fingers faster than you can pick it up. My father never learned this. Fortune in Rome never lasts. There is no peace—nothing grows old.

No one proved this more than Vitellius who, in the tenth month, found that the people had grown tired of him. He tried to buy the hearts of Rome but their price was too high to pay for long. A general of greater renown, of richer taste, of humbler origins, took Vitellius's place. His claim made him the fourth man to call himself Caesar that year alone. Dethroned, Vitellius was paraded through the streets in a red bathrobe. People jeered, threw things at him, and spat all sorts of wicked names.

I didn't hear this. I wasn't around to see it. The day Vitellius was toppled, a list was printed and "Tertius Suetonius" was on it. All those who marched close to Vitellius, with names who were known, were wanted men. It was a very complete list—someone must have blabbed.

I fled, quick as I could, on an aging stallion which I filched from a post where it was tied outside a drinking hall. I had no time to consult the Gaul, who happened to be away. A nameless foreigner, he was not on the list.

I was a mile out when the gates shut behind me. I rode that stallion as hard as I could. With no real aim, the roads from Rome led me North. When I reached Germania, I stopped at the border river. The horse would go no further.

I'd left my father's gold in Rome with the Gaul. There'd been no time.

I'd little in my pockets when I fled but, on the border, a little can go a long way. I bought a tract of land in the woods, farmable, not far from the river. In time, I paid a few workers to help till. I bought a few pigs. It isn't much. My farm is simple enough that no one bugs me. I always pay my dues.

Not fifty miles from where I've settled is the tower of Gaius Commodus. Through a web of rumor, I heard the fate of that one-eyed bandit.

Gaius had not marched with Vitellius, but his name was on the list. One night, soldiers rolled into his camp. The gracious host, Gaius let them through. They gibbeted him from the tower, leaving his body to hang in the wind. His loose band of brigands and no-goods fled without a fight. Wretched as his tower was, the weight of his corpse was enough to do it in. It collapsed three days later, burying the cursed cave and all its wine. No one has since reclaimed the fort. I pray no one ever does.

It is a lonely life I live on the frontier. There is nothing for me back in Rome and only that vast waste beyond. I've thought about taking a wife. To have some kids running around would make a change.

A rough road bisects my farm. I watch it in the late afternoon when the work is done, looking south. I'm not one to make up things, or hang on hopes, but from some aching part, I know what I want to see—a lone rider, kicking up dust in his haste, with hair raven-dark, calves gripping the stirrups, and eyes weighty with riddle.

Edges

Don Brittnacher

Frontiers abound for those who have found
That contentment isn't enough.
Bored of the same and tired of the tame
In a world made small with stuff.

We build rooms for treasure and hoard without measure,
Our dwellings filled high to the sky.
No room for exploring, our trinkets adoring,
Collecting without asking why.

Is there nothing more? What are we living for?
It all seems a senseless waste.
Our lives could be rich, if we'd purge the itch,
To amass things in mindless haste.

When we go to the edges, to the crossings and ledges,

Don Brittnacher

To places where cultures collide,
With comfort behind us and nothing to blind us,
We gaze to the other side.

The boundaries, frontiers, when we go without fears,
Are magical, wonderful places.
With opened eyes, we soon realize
The richness in these special spaces.

It's not profit, nor fame, nor winning the game
That people remember us for.
It's the warmth that we give by the way that we live—
Open arms, open heart, nothing more.

The Last Gunfight

Eric Reuter

The old man rode his horse, listening to the rhythmic sounds of its hooves trotting upon the earth. As he scanned his surroundings, his eyes caught the remains of a wagon. The wood was rotting and the metal frame rusted. He began to reminisce about how the land was harsh and untamed. Some days it was a struggle to survive thirst, starvation, or the blazing heat from the sun. Beasts ranging from the mightiest grizzly bear to a simple snake bite could kill you. Even the water could reduce the strongest man to that of a crying infant. Many attempted to make a living out here, many did not survive. It was said that those who could endure such hardships could never be killed. Like a piece of raw iron heated and pounded on until it was forged into hardened steel.

His concentration was broken by the train whistle. Looking ahead, he grumbled as he approached the town. He remembered when it was nothing more than an outpost. Now it was a thriving community. Riding through the main street, the old man glanced left and right at what others deemed progress. Carriages were becoming mechanized using clockwork gears and steam.

Manual farming equipment was now becoming automated. Food and clean water, which were once a struggle to come by, were now as accessible as the air around them. Even beasts of burden were being replaced by ones made of iron and steel. Glancing at the people in their fancy clothes and automated machines, the old man could tell that not one of them had gone through the same trials he did.

"Whatever happened to the old ways?" the old man muttered to himself as he stopped his horse in front of the general store.

He tied his horse and walked through the door to find a father and son buying supplies. He recognized them. They had just moved there and were struggling to get their farm off the ground. He paid them no mind as he went about his shopping. He heard the door open again and saw three men dressed in fine attire walk in. They were laughing at something. All three wore bowler hats, silk vests, shined boots, and fine tailored suits. One had slick blonde hair, one had a burly mustache, and the other had a distinguishable scar going down his left eye. The three fell silent when they saw the father and son.

The one with the scar sneered as he approached the pair, "Well, well, well, if it isn't McFarley. How is that poor excuse of a farm you're running? Grow anything yet?" They all laughed as the mustached gentleman continued, "Can you believe he still uses live animals and hand tools to plow?" Suddenly, the blonde haired man slugged the father in the stomach, making him drop to his knees. His son began to cry as he tried to help his father.

"When are you going to get with the times and stop making our town look so foolish," the man continued. "This isn't the Old Frontier anymore. Without modernizing, you are doomed to fail."

The words fell upon the old man. He looked at the father and son, their sun-kissed skin, blistered hands, and clothing that had been mended countless times. His gaze returned to the three bullies. *These punks have never worked hard their entire lives,* he thought. Though he barely knew the pair, something deep down told him he had to intervene.

The one with the blonde hair was about to kick the father when he felt a hand grab onto his shoulder. He was spun around and was met with the clenched fist of the old man hitting him square in the jaw. The man stumbled to the ground as his friends attempted to stop his fall.

The blonde haired gent placed a hand on his red jaw as he spat, "What the hell was that for? Who are these wretches to you, you old fossil?"

The old man squared his shoulders and locked his eyes with the man. "They are nothing to me. But don't go insulting the way a man chooses to live his life. Especially when the one doing the insulting has done nothing but sit on their ass and count money all day."

The three stared at the old man, bewildered by his statement. Once the shock wore off, their brows furrowed, their faces reddened with anger. McFarley coughed as he got to his feet with the help from his son. He stared at the old man. He was about to say something when he saw the old man flick his head, signaling that he should leave. He gave a nod and escorted his son out of the store.

"Now where do you think you are going?" the man with the scar said but he was cut off by a swift punch to his soft belly. He coughed and wheezed as he collapsed to the ground.

The one with the mustache stood there, stunned by the strength of the old man. Coming back to his senses, he rushed to his friends and helped them up. The old man stared at the bullies. He had dealt with these types of pests before, rich men who thought their wealth gave them power.

"Now, this is how things are going to go," the old man stated, "You are going to pay for McFarley's supplies, apologize, and leave them alone from now on."

"This isn't the Old West. We have other ways that we can settle this," the man with the mustache stated as he started to reach for his pocketbook.

The old man grimaced. He walked over to him, knocked the pocketbook out of his hand and slugged him in the face. Blood dripped from his broken nose as he wailed in pain.

"Now I don't like repeating myself but since you all don't seem too bright I'll say it one more time. Pay that family, apologize, and leave them alone."

"And what if we refuse?" the one with the scar spat.

"Then we can take this outside and settle this matter the old-fashioned way." The old man pulled back his coat, revealing the pistol strapped to his hip.

The three glanced down at the weapon. The leather holster was cracked. The patina on the pistol was faded and they thought they saw rust on parts of it. The wood grips had long lost their polish and looked like they could split at any moment.

The one with the scar started to laugh, "You think you can beat us with that rusty piece of metal?"

The old man smiled, "I *know* I can beat all three of you." He turned and walked out of the store.

The three men were taken aback by this turn of events. They stared at each other as if waiting for the other to give the appropriate response. The blonde haired and mustached gentlemen nursed their injuries. They stared at each other, clearly not wanting this conflict to continue any further.

They turned to the man with the scar. He was fuming with anger. They could see in his eyes that no amount of talk or reason could dissuade him. He shouted, "If it means putting an old relic like yourself in the ground, then so be it." He threw open the door and followed him outside. The other two, not wanting to seem like cowards, followed their friend.

Passersby noticed the men walking into the street and paused. Murmuring erupted as a crowd formed with the father and son McFarley right in front. The men took their positions. The old man looked at the three. He saw that each one of them had those newfangled clockwork pistols that he had heard about. Each one was polished as if the sun glinted off of them. He could see the gears and mechanisms creak and clack as the men readied them. People said that those guns could fire rounds faster than any conventional weapon known to man.

The crowd grew silent. The only sound that could be heard was the ticking of the town's clock. The big hand rested one minute before the next hour. People glanced back and forth, wondering who would win. The gears of the clock began to turn. The big hand began to move. Before the first chime of the bell could be heard:

BANG! BANG! BANG!

Smoke filled the air between the duelists. The crowd looked on, in stunned silence, as all of the men remained standing. A moment passed, but it felt like an eternity to everyone else. Suddenly, the three men swayed as they collapsed to the ground. The old man let out a snort as he holstered his gun.

He walked over to the three dead men. Rummaging through their pockets he pulled out each of their billfolds. Glancing over to the side he saw the McFarley's. Walking over to them, he handed the father the money without saying a word. He looked down at the boy. He saw both envy and terror in his eyes. *Reminds me a lot of me…when I was younger,* the old man thought.

Reaching down, he undid his gun belt and tossed it to him. The boy looked at it in surprise as he glanced back at the old man. Before he could say anything, the old man walked up to him, knelt down, and said, "Embrace the new…but never forget the old ways."

The boy seemed confused at first but as he stared longer into the old man's eyes, the message sunk in. He furrowed his brow, squared his jaw, and nodded as his grip on the pistol and belt tightened. The crowd dispersed. They still talked about what they had just witnessed and some questioned whether to call the authorities. As they murmured amongst themselves, nobody noticed as the old man slipped away.

The old man wandered into a deserted alley. Moving his hand from his side, he saw that it was covered in blood. *Looks like one of those little punks managed to get me,* he thought as he slumped to the ground.

"Well, the old ways may be coming to a close…but at least I gave them all one more story to tell," he said as he smiled, closed his eyes, and the last breath left his body.

West of Light

Sylvia Coopman

That miserable bell tinkled as the heavy door opened with too much ease. A woman with a young face and wind-whipped hair walked through, dust whirling around her skirt. She held her straw hat on and a basket on her elbow. The woman fought to close the door against the nasty weather. She walked over to the counter, her heels clicking at every step. She pointed toward where I stood tall and asked the shopkeeper how much I was.

The scruffy shopkeeper gave her a steep price and a smug smile. She looked exasperated but paid anyway. The woman turned with a frown, ripped me off the shelf, and walked out the door.

Her hand was warm, warmer than the sun that greeted us through the thick, tan clouds. She threw me in the basket and tucked a worn handkerchief on top, although I was still poking out. I took in the surroundings as much as I could. Strong winds blew loose sand and dirt all around, so I couldn't see beyond a couple of feet. In the basket below me were a few apples, carrots, and eggs. Walking as fast as she could, the woman grimaced and gripped her hat tight.

We soon came upon a building, but only when we got closer did I realize it was a house. From what I could see, it was a large, log house with a small barn behind it, and both held sun damage. Sand was piled at the base of the door, a result of the sandstorm. The woman, struggling to open the door with my basket *and* her hat, kicked away the built-up sand.

Once inside, the woman leaned against the door and breathed a sigh of relief. She set the basket down on a table and put the others in their places. She stuck me in a brass patina and carried me to a desk in an office. The room's walls were almost completely lined with bookcases, and more than half of them were filled. Various chairs were placed throughout the room, which was devoid of life. Everything except the desk I was on, wore a thin layer of dust. I nestled into my holder as much as I could.

About midday, the woman returned to the room with a duster and her husband. He was tall, slender, and clean-shaven, with very blond hair. The woman thanked him for helping with some chores. When she reached to dust a shelf, he approached behind her, wrapped his arms around her waist, and kissed her behind the ear.

He murmured something in her ear; she gasped and giggled his name. Luke. Luke picked her up by her waist. She yelped and dropped the duster. They both chuckled as he carried her out of the room. I didn't see them for the rest of the day. Luke didn't stay the night, though. Thought this to be odd, but perhaps he had evening work.

The next day, Luke came home at noon. He helped her with chores around the house. He talked about the East Coast and how good life was there. But he mostly just tried to get her into bed. And he didn't stay the night.

A night later, when Luke had left, the woman set foot in my room and finally, finally, lit my wick for the first time. She sat in the chair that was too big for her, opened a tidy drawer, and took out a few slips of paper. She sighed, grabbed a pen, and wrote:

Dear Beloved Henry,

I had no thought to be this alone when you left me for War and Mr. Crockett. Without you, this house be too empty, my steps echo around me, I suppose a mockery to your absence. Two days ago, a sandstorm almost took me to my knees, but still I went out. I pray God for your safety and wish you hadn't left me so. I worry muchly you won't return home. Mrs. Johnson said that in the war for our independence, her father, John, lost both his legs by artillery. I hope to God that won't be so, my love. Rumors I've heard say the Mexicans aren't taking prisoners.

She wrote long and hard about a coyote snacking on their livestock, that Mr. Johnson now had her favorite squash seeds, and other mundane things. My holder caught the drippings as my height diminished. She signed it with a flourish, "Your loving wife, Betty."

Luke was not her husband?

She laid her head down in her arms and stared at my fire. It was strange, but I liked it. Her face held nothing. My light caught her wedding ring, and the gem centered in the band sparkled. Although a little unnerved, I was glad to provide something more than light. She folded the letter and put it in an envelope. She blew out my flame and left the room.

Another week went on. Luke still came at noon and left at dusk. Betty had yet to write any more letters to Henry during this time. Now at about half my original height, I watched as Betty stepped into the room, sat again in the oversized chair, and wrote:

Dear Henry,

Oh, when are you coming home, dear? I do hope you're alright. I bought squash seeds the day before yesterday. They should be planted by the time you arrive back home, since Luke has been a fine help around the ranch.

Betty also mentioned tedious things, like tending livestock and the house. She again signed the letter with love. My wick was not alight for long.

Over a fortnight, these letters became more distant and less romantic. Luke was here more often in the early morning and stayed late into the night with Betty, in Henry's bed.

At the start of the third week, he convinced Betty to go back East with him. He'd also said something about not wanting to be here when the war came. She'd mentioned still loving Henry, but Luke waved it off. It was a short battle between the two.

Almost to the end of my wick, she wrote one last letter to Henry:

Henry,

I'm sorry.

Goodbye,

Elisabeth

Elisabeth tucked the folded note into an envelope, slipped off her ring, and put it with the letter. She picked up the pen again and wrote "Henry" on the front in neat calligraphy. She snuffed out my light and left the dark room with a delighted smile.

I sat for another two fortnights. She'd taken the paper and pens with her. Cold snuck its way into the wick at my core, freezing me solid. I was convinced no one would be here for a very long time.

Heavy, uneven steps sounded throughout the house. Someone was here.

A rough, deep voice calling out for Elisabeth. It got louder and closer until the door to the office opened. A dirty, tired, war-worn man with a prominent limp hobbled into the office. This must be Henry.

I was thankful that someone was here, but he wasn't here for me. He was here for his wife. He said her name one last time, almost as an afterthought. Then, in the moonlight, he noticed the letter with his name on it.

Every step was painful for him. One of the unlucky defenders of the Alamo. He shuffled over to the desk and lit my wick with a match.

Henry opened the letter, hands shaking. A look of confusion appeared. It turned into disbelief, and he scoffed. In anguish, he let out a choked sob and collapsed into the chair that fit just right. Then rage. His trembling hands held the delicate letter over my flame. Fire overcame the page as it slowly burned away until there was nothing but ashes. Henry stood completely still, staring at my flame.

His breathing was labored, his fists clenched. With a scream of fury, Henry grabbed the underside of the desk and flipped it on its side. The fall jolted me, having not been moved in a month. The impact knocked me from my holder, making me roll a few feet. Henry continued to destroy the room.

Amazingly, my wick was still lit. I'd stopped rolling under a floor-length curtain behind the desk. The little fire from my cord caught on the curtain, bursting into flames. The fire ate up the curtain. But before any of the burning material covered me, Henry, in his madness, knocked over a bookcase. I was launched toward the middle of the room and my wick went out. It was then that he noticed the fire. The flames had ruined the curtains and spilled onto the ceiling and floor. His smile was vicious.

We watched as the office, which had been home to both of us at one point, burned brilliantly. The pyre spread to the walls of books, devouring them. It crawled closer to me by the floor, relighting my core.

The last I saw of Henry before I melted away, was him marching out of the burning house. His hands curled into fists, the devil perched on his shoulder, and a shadow of fire trailing behind him.

Tomas is a Planet

S. J. Heinz

Condor Transport is a breakout galactic cargo service. A freight moon bus has a human crew of two, the conductor and the engineer. There is a fleet of exactly thirty spacecraft in commission. The vessels are guided remotely to and from their destination. It is anticipated that human passengers will outpace commodity transfers aboard the buses, as transit becomes more affordable and incident-free.

Tomas Gallagher was diagnosed with aphonic autism spectrum disorder at the age of three. The wishy-washy scientific community tried to put a stamp on people like Tomas, but it would not stick. Against quantifiable odds, 26-year-old Tomas aced his tests and was assigned the position as conductor on Condor #27.

Tomas was cerebral, practical, and demanding. He delighted in order and uniformity. He could be persnickety, yet resourceful and attentive to hidden patterns in dot plots, pie charts, and graphs of every imaginable kind. Unlike most of his peers, he could see the trees through the forest.

Tomas used a portable, dialog Talky workstation, preferring it to struggling with actual speech. He chose a dulcet voice, slow and deliberate—similar to the award-winning American actor of Star Trek fame, Leonard Nimoy, who remained a popular icon into the late 21st century. In fact, Talky makers mechanically skyjacked Nimoy's voice and managed to avoid litigation due to the erosion of copyrights since the dawn of social media.

In a rare turn of fate, when a part-time engineer position on Condor #27 became available, Tomas's younger sister, Jody Gallagher Graf, applied. She was unique too. She had an advanced degree in aeronautics and worked at the Washburn Observatory as a data scientist. Jody was over-qualified for her chosen field. But she believed that her marital status and a regulatory system that paved the way for Space Force relatives reduced her odds of ever becoming an astronaut to travel to other planets. The moon bus was her ticket.

The brother-sister team completed over thirty missions before they encountered a stunning trip interruption last year.

"Seat belts?" Tomas keyed into his customized computer. "Outdated. We really don't need them."

"Put yours on anyway!" Jody ordered her superior.

"In case you haven't heard, we glide into outer space nowadays," he said. Because he could be verbose and overly analytic with lightning-fast fingers, Nimoy's speech trailed light years behind the keyboard. "You want to be a stewardess? You are on the wrong aircraft. We may feel some tremors–nothing to be alarmed about."

Jody pinched his arm. Tomas winced. As the vessel prepared for takeoff, she buckled up. Tomas stood in front of the task panel, reading the patterns of activity. It was the same as it should be. There was no person-to-person visual between earth and sky. Tomas liked it that way.

"Have a safe trip, Conductor Gallagher and Engineer Graf," Julia, the dispatcher, gave the standard farewell. "Buckle up, Conductor!"

The pair had long concluded that although they could not see Julia, her ability to monitor them closely with more than human interest indicated that she was not human at all. Unbeknownst to them, the machine had the smoky, contralto voice of Cher Bono Allman, a revered singer and entertainer before the United States of Americas coalition.

"Goodbye!" Tomas said.

"Who does Tomas listen to?" Julia sighed in a tone that anyone who vaguely remembered Cher could imagine pursing her lips and flipping her long black hair over her shoulder.

"No one," Jody returned. "Tomas listens to no one."

Tomas and Jody put their sleek, fiberglass flight helmets on, lowering their noise-blocking flaps over their ears. Tomas's hat was black with the orange silhouette of a soaring raptor; Jody's had a gleaming purple finish.

They applied their oxygen lip locks, developed by Body Shield which switched gears from athletic teeth guards to innovative outer-space attire. With a deep breath, the devices snapped into place. Tomas had a set of fangs on his mouthpiece, Jody's had big red lips. They looked at each other and giggled.

The digital timekeeper counted down. There were flashing red letters reminding the crew to "fasten your seatbelts." Tomas wondered when that piece of obsolete advice would disappear. He grasped wall handles on either side of the travel monitor, prepared for some light choppiness. Takeoff went well, as he expected. The mouthpieces could be removed now, but like a bandage, it could hurt when taken off, leaving skin impressions.

As a fuel-saving measure, the global standard remains for air vessels to float in the exosphere. They had an hour layover before proceeding to the moon. This didn't make sense to Tomas, but he wasn't a rocket scientist. He surmised that it was likely more of a logistical measure to avoid collisions.

It was time to bring Peet and Penny out of their pet carriers. Recently acquired from a lab rescue through Creature Care of Wisconsin, the nearly naked, desexed cavies were of a type called skinny guinea pigs. They were affectionate, hairless tribbles. Tomas rewarded his stowaways with timothy grass pellets. He knew full well that having pets aboard the freight ship was frowned upon.

An amenity afforded the crew was to raise the window guards to view the other aircrafts, satellites, and space junk—particularly the largest deposit of garbage, the Icarus Dump. Sometimes the smaller luxury aircrafts sailed so close that you could make out waving people. Tomas watched the people while they waited, comfortable with them at a distance. He would wave a small United States of Americas flag on a stick and flash the lights as much as anybody else. International sky troopers don't mind a little fun, but if they need to, they had small crafts that could dart in and out of traffic, latching on to an offending vehicle.

Tethering during the waiting period is a popular pastime for some of those with a daredevil streak. Condor Transport forbid it, but Tomas did it at least a dozen times. Jody had been enticed to do it too. Putting on the baggy, foil-like under suit is a bit of a chore. A vacuum sucks the suit skintight. Then there is the overlay. The walking suit is slightly less cumbersome than those worn by the original astronauts, but young spacewalkers push for fashion choices in gear and often advertise their trip sponsors.

It is expected that low-orbit tethering should yield a certain number of deaths each year. The Dump is designed like a giant magnet to attract man-made articles devoid of activity, but on some occasions, space waste escapes while smaller manned vessels or an occasional tether are caught in its vacuum. The risk of a space walker being killed by the Dump is miniscule, but most of the bodies of reckless tethers are retrieved within its borders.

"Do you want to walk?" Tomas asked, scratching the implanted tattoo on his left shoulder.

"No, Tomas," Jody scolded. "And stop scratching! If you wreck it, you won't be able to get through security."

"I never heard of anyone wrecking it," he replied, typing his response with one hand while scratching the spot with the other. "That's illogical."

"Okay, Spock! But, when we get to the moon, you are going to see a doctor." Jody looked at his skin. She found her soothing lip moisturizer, applied some to the palm of her hand, and then to the inflammation. "I think you're allergic to Peet and Penny. Now, stop scratching it," she ordered, refastening the shoulder access on his flight suit. "I'm watching you."

The shoulder tattoos revealed their shared lineage, although the naked eye could not. This is something more important to the powers-that-be than the people branded with them.

The hour-long wait in the parking belt was nearly intolerable. Tomas was fidgety. He finally settled on looking through the cargo manifest—to him a good read. Jody was sketching on a doodle pad device. After twenty minutes, she slid a button to the piano setting and played a familiar tune with one hand. She sang:

Tomas is a planet

Furthest from the sun

An atmosphere as thick as mud

He listens to no one!

Tomas is a planet

He orbits around me

Few will ever get inside

So let this fella be!

They both laughed, but as Jody continued to play it, this time with the setting on classic guitar, Tomas put his helmet back on and lowered the earflaps. They were not children anymore, but now in their twenties. They were siblings with a bond frozen in time.

"Something's not right," Tomas alerted his sister, noting abnormalities in the screens while conducting his standard readings.

Jody joined him in front of the navigation screen which Tomas had manipulated into four separate panels. The pair observed a diagram of the Condor. A blue aura indicating the perimeter of the protective force shield. There was a disturbance at the rear of the ship. It registered as an object of no concern. Likely escaped space garbage.

Tomas pressed another button to pull up the weather reports. There was nothing alarming. Yet, everyone knew a solar burst was about to hit over Asia Minor in the next 48 hours.

"The hold has been compromised," Tomas continued, returning to the graphics. He pointed to the irregularity. "Glitch one–space junk. Or we have been hit." Then he returned to the diagram of the Condor, keying, "Glitch two—mega solar flare not predicted."

"You're right! The flare should be shown. Maybe the information changed?" But Jody knew that would be an impossible oversight. "Meteorologists are basically a bunch of weathermen–far from perfect. Worst case scenario, we get a layover at the Horus Moon Base," she said. "I'll run down and take a look at the hull."

Deciding to trust the Space Weather Prediction Center, Jody calmly shimmied out of her flight suit and into the foil-like layer of her space suit. She opted to wear the skintight vestment and her mouthpiece. She opened the hatch, gave Tomas a thumbs up and descended into the freight hold.

Tomas considered the readings out of the ordinary. He struggled to remain calm and rational, calling to memory comforting visions of the beautiful Wisconsin woodlands and its giant beaver-guinea pigs. He clutched his hands as a means of calming himself by applying pressure to sensory points. It always worked.

With less than five minutes to relaunch, Jody emerged.

"Some blankety-blank scraped our side," she reported. "No structural damage. Too light to sound an alarm. I suppose it could have been missed before takeoff. What's going on?" She nodded towards the control room windows. "Nobody is moving! If we don't get this show on the road, we won't make it to the Moon Station at Horus on schedule."

Tomas was in control again, running the calculations to leave on schedule by overriding Condor dispatch. Other ships were deviating from the line, as navigators ignored an orderly removal.

"Condor 27, come in," Julia from dispatch interrupted. "Conductor Gallagher, Engineer Graf, please come in."

"Damn, she caught us," Jody groaned. "Engineer Graf and Conductor Gallagher, Condor #27, go ahead, Navigator."

"Abort mission," Julia said. "Space Enforcement Officers are evacuating all human occupants in the immediate exosphere over Asia Minor. Mega solar flare approaching ahead of schedule. Gear up and be ready to go." Then without further warning, it said, "Putting the Condor in park—in three, two, one! The ship is now parked."

Tomas was livid. Julia, an artificial intellect, had not allowed them time enough to initiate their plan.

"Any questions?" it belatedly inquired.

"Because of the solar flare?" Tomas asked, in his Leonard Nimoy voice.

"Yes, Conductor. Mega solar flare. Ten times larger than Earth. Prepare to take cover at Gamma Global. Communications expected to be interrupted. We will resume operations as soon as possible."

Then, a built-in feature to relax the doomed was initiated–poetry readings with classical string music. Device trickery! To end the annoying, disingenuous communication, Jody reached over Tomas and typed, "Copy that, Navigator."

The solar storm was going to be a big one. If all went as Julia said, most of the travelers would survive without major radiation poisoning. Gamma Global Space Station would be a safe haven. By all accounts, Peet and Penny would be safe in the cosmic-ray tolerant module generally reserved for clothing and other personal effects. It was into this compartment they were quickly deposited.

A sleek, fast-flying, twelve-seater Space Enforcement vehicle docked with the Condor. Tomas and Jody saw the distraught faces of the passengers who had removed their helmets with their lip locks in place, waiting for the shuttle to fly them out of the direct path of the violent flare.

"One seat left," the pilot announced.

"You should go first," Tomas said.

"It is protocol for the conductor to evacuate," Jody protested.

"The pilot will be back for me," Tomas replied with resolve. "Go! I will be right behind you."

Jody could see that Tomas would rather die than get inside with those strange people.

"All right, both of us will wait for the next shuttle."

But Tomas would not have it. He shoved her towards the loading chute, and Jody reluctantly took a seat in the transporter. She watched him wave his United States of Americas flag, smiling like a loon.

Extending her thumb, her pointer and her little finger, Jody pressed her last two fingers into the palm of her hand until it hurt. The universal symbol "I love you."

In another moment, the craft sped away.

The super solar burst was already interrupting data and causing transmission failures. The magnitude of the sun flare would be the highest yet recorded.

When the rescue runs were completed, Tomas had not been collected.

Playing with Matches

S. J. Heinz

The value of the boreal forest in the Chequamegon National Forest in North Central Wisconsin was only recently recognized. Now under protection by international law, unless you have a legacy clause to remain within its boundaries or have an admittance permit, you are there illegally.

The territory was heavily logged in the mid-1850s but a hundred-year reprieve allowed the woodland to rebound. Before its legal status as a significant source of North America's oxygen supply, it was largely underappreciated. In fact, an animal compound at LaBelle Falls was the dumping ground for university laboratory animals not marked for adoption or euthanasia. Their numbers remain sensibly small, making the caretaker's wards unique, even valuable.

A trust fund set aside for the upkeep of a vacation lodge, a hobby farm, outbuildings, and an additional seventeen hectares of regenerated timber enables the foundling program to exist in perpetuity. Timber baron Maurice LaBelle would be rolling in his grave if he could see what has become of his up-north getaway.

It is sheer serendipity that a former taxidermy workshop became housing to a menagerie of castoff animals. When the last of the LaBelle bloodline selected expedited euthanasia in 2032, ownership passed to the private Collier College for Mammalian Research in Upper Michigan.

The retired lab animals are kept in a massive taxidermy outbuilding erected over one-hundred-fifty years earlier. The workshop has its original concrete flooring. From brown porcelain baseboards, ceramic tiles line the walls to the halfway point. Below their cap rails, at sporadic intervals, handmade relief tiles of creatures of every sort from fish to bears enchant the beholder. Ignorant of the organic splatter that once may have covered the walls up to those pretty tiles, one cannot resist running their fingers over their cool rippled surfaces.

LaBelle Falls was never visited by the members of the college executive board of directors but the starving institution embraced the gift. Due to the donor's final wishes, Collier could not legally sell or develop the Wisconsin estate but it could get a hefty percentage of the trust fund's annual interest.

Management of the lumberjack's cottage fell to Dr. Robert Dunwiddie. Dunwiddie's wife, Mary Jane, became the property caretaker.

"I don't care how often we say that we are not an animal shelter or a wildlife refuge, a week doesn't go by that we don't get a box of kittens or a hawk with a damaged wing," Mary Jane complained to her husband, pressing the edge of the foldable communicator to her chest. "On Saturday, I have to hire a van to ship the animals to Rhinelander. It's too much," she sobbed, running a hand through her shortly-cropped blonde hair. "When are you coming home, Bob? You once told me that we are less than two-hundred miles apart. It wouldn't be an issue. Now you are home only once a month." She threw his promise in his face. "I can't do it alone."

It was late summer and the visiting Gallagher kids ran into the kitchen with the screen door banging behind them. Their bathing suits smelled of earthy rotten eggs. They were laughing and tugging on a beach towel. Their mother Victoria was on their heels, begging them to stop.

"Well, the kids are back," Mary Jane said. "Guess I'll talk to you tomorrow. Love you too," she said, half-heartedly.

Folding the communicator phone, she put it in the pocket of her smock. It was hard not to smile at the giggling little boy and his younger sister as they ignored their mother's pleas.

"Back outside!" Victoria ordered. As the children raced out the kitchen door, she called out to their father, "Watch the kids! I'm going to help feed the critters!"

"Thanks, I am almost ready. I just have to fix Peanut's dish," Mary Jane said.

Peanut was the only bird in the zookeeper's menagerie. A Eurasian jackdaw. Two-hundred grams of feathers and feist. The jackdaw is in the same family tree as the common crow. He showed an astounding capacity for self-learning and vocalization. Peanut had a firm association with words and phrases in English, Latin, Spanish, and Japanese. Before his brain tissue could be studied, a team member at Collier sent him to the sanctuary. But, at five years old, Peanut was already a senior citizen and given many extra privileges.

"I'll take care of the guinea pigs," Victoria offered.

The scent of the lake beach wafted through the air again. It was Tomas.

"Guinea pigs!" he squealed.

"Where did you come from, my love?" Victoria purred with pride. "Sure, you can feed the guinea pigs."

Peanut was not in his cage. Rather than clip the wings of a bird that lived to cartwheel in the air, the bird was allowed his freedom a few hours each day.

Taking full advantage, a black blaze of happiness darted to and fro speaking its native language.

"Kak, kak!"

"Peanut!" Tomas shouted, covering his ears. "Peanut, stop!"

Guinea pigs and the jackdaw were great speech motivators for Tomas, who was labeled an autistic nonverbal at the age of three. In a landmark time when a human being's net worth was determined by genetics and social equity, his story is written in indelible pigment embedded in his juvenile shoulder. With a mop of red hair and green eyes that never fixed on strangers, his hereditary map leaned towards his father's Irish heritage. His diet consisted of French fries, frankfurters, and peanut butter sandwiches. But during this particular summer visit, Tomas was influenced by the menus of the inmates and he began to eat apples, bananas, mandarin oranges, raisins, and sunflower seeds.

The Three Pigs were special because they were produced in laboratory Petri dishes. Peruvian guinea pigs were methodically crossbred with the North American beaver. What was that research team thinking? Hands down, those animals required the most care. Weighing close to twenty kilograms each, the not-so-little critters looked like colorful beavers. Originally there had been eight of them. They were designed for a fur jacket but the customer decided against the patchwork look and the animals were rendered useless. Only four of them made it to Creature Care.

Other than being cute, the Three Pigs had few redeeming features. Of course, Tomas adored Eeny, Meeny, and Miny. There had been a Moe, the only male. He was electrocuted when he gnawed through an active hybrid electrical cord during one of his escapes. Mary Jane did her best to keep the creatures entertained in the safe confines of their glass enclosures.

That particular day, Tomas took charge of the pigs. He delivered carrot tops and an armful of natural apple wood spheres woven by his grandmother at her home along the Chequamegon. His mother tottered a birch stump into their main play area.

Mary Jane's emotions were tested as she moved amid her hapless charges, including two Capuchin monkeys and an old Bonobo chimpanzee chattering on a Fisher-Price talking tablet. Sally, the Bonobo, incorporates sign language too. A unicorn, created from feral ponies from the Virginia side of Assateague Island, was surgically altered as an embryo to produce a horn on its forehead. Fortunately, the horn sheds in late winter.

The singing Long Evans rats had a repertoire of nursery songs produced with a series of deliberate chirps, grunts, and whistles. "Old MacDonald Had a Farm" is the seemingly favorite, and the accidental progeny easily adapt it.

Mary Jane wondered how much research money had been wasted on these enterprises. Teaching institutions frolicked in unknown territories, frivolously blending nucleic acids of unrelated species. Ultimately, playing with matches.

Looking upon Tomas that afternoon reinforced Mary Jane's belief that scientific research would be better spent on learning two-way communication with a child like him. But the Patient-Doctor Act, part of the early euthanasia option, favored alleviating the problem in its early stages. Although natural human offspring are preferred by most couples, if parents like Tomas Gallagher's XX and XY partners choose to shoulder the burden of natural imperfections, the medical community presents an obligatory warning and a way out. To refuse the solution forfeits social responsibility.

To Mary Jane, who had no children, the Gallagher kids were the most fascinating of all creatures.

When four-year-old Jody arrived that summer, she insisted on measuring the feed for the animals. As her enthusiasm abated, she declared, "Sorry,

Auntie Mary Jane, I am busy learning today." She wandered off with a pencil, a paper, and a digital ruler, deciding to draw and measure the animals instead.

Unlike Tomas, Jody was babbling since she was three months old and reading at two years old. Left to its own accord, spontaneous genetics can cook an unusual soup. Jody's hereditary scan showed that she favored her mother's Indigenous North American and Teutonic European genes. She has dark skin, black hair, and a low-level deformity called heterochromia, having one hazel eye and one brown eye.

While unsupervised, the children roughhouse across the artificial turf and foliage in the resort's atrium. Over the course of time, an Egg Harbor taxidermist built a diorama. The artist's vision entices the mischievous pair to reconfigure the embalmed rabbits and squirrels and to hop onto the backs of the mother black bear and her cub. Sometimes Jody hid in the branches of the living cottonwood which, to this day, grows in the center of the exhibit. And long after each visit, the caretaker found polymer dinosaurs hidden there.

In the summer evenings, the Gallagher children like to sit side-by-side on a reclining lawn chair to gaze at the stars. Surrounded by a symphony of crickets, and the rare, comforting sounds of croaking toads in the nearby brook, they talk about flying in spaceships, visiting the moon, and other planets. Tomas, of course, uses Anselm sign language and some verbal words when he is forced to. Their parents challenge them to memorize the constellation maps, and they are able to identify several of the star patterns in the Northern Hemisphere.

"Ursa Minor," Jody said.

"Grrr Brrr," Tomas replied, pointing to the Great Bear.

"Very good, Tomas," she clapped.

But summers always end, and farewells are often bittersweet. While the Gallaghers were loading up their potato-mash fueled vehicle to leave that year, the children wandered off to say goodbye to the animals. No one knew who left the barn door and the guinea pig enclosures ajar, but everyone assumed it was Tomas.

A cursory review of the inventory showed that Peanut and the Three Pigs were gone.

Plover folks never heard of LaBelle Creature Care. Bernice Weber only knew that she had a chit-chatty blackbird visiting her bird feeder. After it ate the choicest seeds, it demanded an apple.

When the stunned woman did not respond quickly enough, Peanut asked, "Hablasss essspanol?"

The widow Weber asked her neighbors if they had seen or heard of this bird. They had not, suspecting that Bernice's days at home alone were numbered. When it started to get colder, the talking bird darted inside the open patio door and decided to stay. The unsuspecting woman had never had a pet bird, and she found that it was a tad more demanding than her late husband had been. But she was no longer solitary or unengaged at Vineyard Drive.

The fate of the Three Pigs is troubling. While Eeny was found within an hour, Meeny came home after a few days hungry and pregnant. Miny was never found.

A dozen of Miny's progeny have been trapped on the Wisconsin River. And on the northside of Thunder Lake, some interlopers claim to have heard the whistles of the resourceful Beaver Pigs singing "Old MacDonald Had a Farm."

According to scientific experts, insemination should not have occurred outside of a laboratory. Yet, to this day, beaver-like creatures of various hues are found in the vicinity of the Chequamegon Forest, leaving trails of tree stumps in their wake.

The Lady of the Wood

First performed October 2023 at The Fox Delight fantasy ball
Rebecca M. Zornow

"Well, can we finally be done with this?"

I looked up from my perch on the steps in surprise. I had sought out the moment to watch the proceedings of the gathering alone and hadn't expected to be followed.

Around me, fairy queens danced with men in long cloaks and Mother Earth held a small crowd enthralled by the bar. The noise of the throng enveloped me in a bubble of reality, a half step away from the surreal events of the night.

"What do you mean?" I asked my husband. We were in the middle of a party, one more intricate and lively than our own wedding. The celebration was hardly done and besides, I expected him to help clean up at the end.

"You know that thing where you think that you're not successful and cast doubt onto your projects when in reality you're a rockstar? After a night like this one, can we be done with that?"

I threw my head back and laughed. I had just been thinking along the same lines—not a surprise as the theme had been a constant in our conversations ever since I decided to become a writer.

It started when my sister slid a notebook across the table and told me we could write a book together. I looked at her, dumbfounded. A book? The two of us? I was a huge reader, even earned myself an English degree, but the idea to write something longer than a term paper had honestly never popped into my head. I figured that was something other people did. People who deserved the freedom of creativity.

Over the next five years, we wrote a memoir together. The words inside could pierce your skin and web their way to your heart. I understood more about the person I had grown up with, looked again at the complexity of childhood, and learned to tell a story. Yet the manuscript was flawed. We pitched it relentlessly and eventually set it aside when it was clear the timing wasn't right. The book went into a drawer. Waiting to come out.

But that book made me a writer. And writing is what writers do. So, I wrote another book. That book failed to lift off, so I wrote another book, a book about aliens and gender that was so viscerally me I needed to speak those words to the world, my first published book. I kept writing and wrote two more books and, more astonishingly, sold thousands of copies. My sister and I started a book coaching company to support other writers with a fondness for magical, weird, and futuristic tales.

On paper, I was a success. In my head, I floundered between sublime creative confidence and, well, the fear that everything I had ever created was worthless and all the things I had ever written were complete rubbish. Even as I came to know myself better than ever, it was as if the hardest bits were sequestered firmly into one corner of my brain. I would take those ugly bits out and spin them in my fingers when I had a spare five minutes and an inkling of doubt.

The venture that haunted me most was an LLC I started with both my sister and brother; the purpose of the company was to run science fiction and fantasy conventions in our hometown. It seemed like the perfect mesh of our shared interests and we hoped there was an audience waiting for something like this to happen. So, after filing all the paperwork, we went into planning mode, even got as far as putting the finishing touches on the large-scale event when the pandemic hit.

We delayed the event. Then canceled. Waited. And three-years later had an LLC that had done nothing, achieved nothing, felt a little too much like a mirror. I didn't like looking in that direction.

And then one day I saw a video of friends enjoying a hobbit party in a field. Soon after, on a walk, a story idea popped into my head. The Lady of the Wood and her missing brother. One dark night, the Lady arrives at The Fox Delight, a magical tavern that appears in Appleton, WI every sixth full moon. She tells the magical folk her brother is missing. The crowd is moved. Until they learn what she wants is not her brother safely returned, but vengeance.

The idea captivated me. I couldn't stop thinking about this Lady, but more than that, I couldn't stop thinking about all the people who lived in my town that were hungry for a bit of magic in their life. The combination of a story and a need made me bold.

It took months to orchestrate the event. We hired actors, evaluated venues, pulled together a meager budget. Details started to coalesce. Guests would get in with a magical coin. Between live performances, they would go on side quests up and down the avenue to solve the mystery of the Lady of the Wood and her missing brother.

As the date approached, I began to have bouts of doubt. Who was I to plan a magical fantasy ball? I wasn't a master cosplayer. Who was I to write a script? I had never even taken part in a play besides a single Christmas pageant scene.

If there's one thing I do, though, it's follow through. I seem to learn more and more that following through is the single most important attribute of my creative process. So, I would stick it out and see what happened. If I lost ten grand or accidentally burned down the venue with hundreds of battery-powered candles…well, that was a chance I would have to take.

Besides, I was an important part of the night: I had cast myself as Delilah Honeydew, owner of The Fox Delight fantasy tavern, to give me a reason to make announcements throughout the evening and prod the guests along on the adventure.

As Delilah, I set up the ballroom with my brother and sister, and then painted my skin yellow and put on a pair of fawn ears. It was showtime.

The night of, at six o'clock sharp, I nearly bit my tongue when two women arrived in ball gowns, eager to come in out of the cold. Soon after, elves arrived. Women in crowns and wings. A monster or two. I had done it. I had convinced mild-mannered citizens to come out in fantasy dress and go on an adventure with me.

But that was only the beginning.

The Lady of the Wood Performance Part 1

LADY enters

THE LADY OF THE WOOD [to a random person]: Well, aren't you going to announce me? Never mind, I'll do it myself.

LADY [to room]: Townsfolk, your Lady of the Wood has arrived. Quiet your jests, still your revelry. I have arrived with a matter of greatest importance. I do not like to come to these…establishments, especially rooted in human territory, but I have no choice. My brother has been missing a week today.

BARD comes to center of the room

THE BARD: My Lady, Felix the Bard at your service. You will not find your brother here this night. I am sure you must be greatly worried for him but—

LADY: I am not worried for his sake.

BARD: Not worried for your brother? Who's been missing a week? I am certain I remember your younger sibling here one night, surrounded by a crowd as he detailed an adventure you took together to quell the Beast of Bray Road. In Elkhorn, Wisconsin, wasn't it? Is this the same brother you speak of?

LADY: It's true…he was once the single person I could trust. But he's been poisoned by this human world. Pokémon Go. BookTok. These so-called heads of cheese. I cannot stomach such things. The human stench spills over to our magical world more every day. You all may be content to mingle with non-magicals, but I still remember a time when Fae ruled these lands in totality.

BARD: Then why have you come, my Lady? I fail to see how we common folk can help one as great as yourself locate a fellow being of immense power, when you yourself have been unable to do so.

LADY: I have not come for my brother. I have come to reclaim what he stole from me.

TELLER stumbles in from the back

FORTUNE TELLER: My Lady, my Lady, I was just in the chamber pot room when I heard that you were here. I see, I see a blue aura. The fates, they *speak* to me! You are worried sick over your missing brother!

BARD and LADY share a look

BARD: *Thatcher*…every vampire, wizard, and knight here knows the Lady is not looking for her brother, but the item he apparently stole.

TELLER: *Bows before the LADY* It would be my great honor to help you, O Majestic One. For I have the gift! The gift of sight. *drops some of his cards and scrambles to pick them up* I see all. I can assist you in finding this-this object.

LADY: An object of extreme importance.

TELLER: Indeed. I can see its powerful aura.

LADY: So, you know where it is?

TELLER: Well, not quite, but I can obviously see that the object is very important!

BARD: Important enough to bring the Lady of the Wood out of her isolated valley. Where is that again? Near Little Lake "But de Mort" [Lake Butte de Morts enunciated].

LADY: Stop that, Bard. You know very well French settlers made up that name. Its proper name is Paehkuahkīhsaeh as the Menominee called it. And what is with that broken lute? Why are you not playing with the others tonight?

BARD: I was nearby, reading the newest book by local author Rebecca M. Zornow. It's science fiction, which is this odd human way of writing about the future–well, forget it. Anyways, I was reading when I was attacked by a dark creature. A creature only one such as yourself could summon. You realize your search for your brother—excuse me, this object—will put the humans of this town in danger.

LADY: It doesn't matter. I need it back!

TELLER: Oh! I see it! I see it, yes, yes, yes. A valuable made of aluminum alloy, magnesium, silicon dioxide, and lithium; a device that will tell you tomorrow's weather and what someone on the other side of Appleton thinks about Bird Scooters on sidewalks—

LADY: I've seen a phone before. Really, are you sure you're one of the magical folk?

BARD: My Lady, Thatcher is one of the best fortune tellers in town.

LADY: Thatcher? An unusual name for a soothsayer.

TELLER: My family runs a prosperous roofing company in town, Dempsey's Roofing. It was always assumed I'd join the family business when I came of age.

LADY: Well, the sight must not be strong in your family if they didn't see you coming. Still, my apologies, Thatcher, that accusation was a low blow. I'm sure one such as yourself will be able to find my lost object.

BARD: And the object in question, my Lady?

LADY: Trust me, you'll know it when you see it.

TELLER: And I also see there's a reward for finding the object. Rent is due you know.

LADY: We'll see about that after it's returned to me. *Looks around the room* I see I will need to help you all along. I will summon forth the details, *spell* it all out for you if I must. *snaps fingers and scrolls appear* You have one and a half hours. I'll return at 8:30. Well? Get to it!

After the performance, my husband and I handed out little scrolls and wax sealed letters to take guests on three side quests. Within fifteen minutes, the ballroom was empty. Everyone was out questing on College Avenue. I grabbed myself a plate of food and sat down heavily, my feet already tired.

I would take tired though. The venue hadn't had its doors locked because I accidentally booked the wrong date. None of the actors had broken a leg. I hadn't tested positive for COVID just hours before the start of the event. Everything was extraordinarily fine.

I took a bite of a Neverwhere Steak Crostini. It was good.

There was movement at my side. It was an actor, the Fortune Teller. He ceremoniously placed a Tarot card on the table. The Wheel of Fortune.

He spoke, his voice deep and languid. "All your dreams will come true."

I wasn't sure if we were still role playing or if this was real life. It was both I suppose. I laid my hand on his sleeve. "I have been waiting to hear that for a *very* long time," I said with all truthfulness.

The Lady of the Wood Part 2

TELLER stands in the center of the room

FORTUNE TELLER: Where is the Lady of the Wood? I have told many fortunes tonight, proven my skill in earnest, but The Lady disappeared some time ago. You? Have you seen the Lady of the Wood? I am certain I can help her if she would just–

The LADY enters the front door with GOUL of SPIRIT WALKER

THE LADY OF THE WOOD: Magic folk of the night, subjects of my domain, I am The Lady of the Wood. You see the power I wield. The darkness that has grown inside of me. Yet, you have spent your time playing games, drinking, gossiping about my private affairs. Enough! If I need to dismantle this town to find what I seek, then I will let lose my beast!

GOUL circles TELLER and snaps his jaws

TELLER: My Lady, there is no need. Please, we are all trying–

LADY: –I care not for tries and attempts. I will have what is mine. Whether the Fox Delight is still standing when I'm done is up to you! My brother is gone. I want him back, safe.

The Bard steps forward, now with elf ears on

BARD/BROTHER: Forgive me the ruse, sister.

Lady: Brother!

BARD: It was a glamor, a simple spell to make me appear differently as long as you were angry with me. And I knew you'd be mad. But, if you can see me, it appears you are less so?

LADY: I thought you were–never mind. *sighs* Go, Goul, it seems you are not needed this night….How could you disappear on me? I thought we were a team. And last time I checked, *you* weren't powerful enough to hide a simple spell from me. What's going on? And this? Working as a lowly singer at The Fox Delight?

BARD: And at The Wood Violet Lounge on Tuesdays.

LADY: But-but *why*? Never mind, I don't care. Where is it?

BARD: You always do this, you hide yourself away in your castle, deigning to go among the people.

TELLER: A reconciliation! I sense a reconciliation.

LADY: I think not. And, brother, are you saying I'm rude?

TELLER: Well, you weren't nice to me. I could have done a reading for you, you know.

LADY: *opens mouth in a pause* Well I suppose I was. But it's because I can't trust anyone. The world is changing. These humans and their AI generators think they run everything. They think they know all when they cannot even keep their woods from burning, their lakes free of pollution, or the ice cream machines working at their fast food establishments! Why have you done this? Why are you taking their side over mine?

Bard removes the item from his pocket

BARD: I'll give back The Heart of the Forest if you rid our streets of dark beings.

LADY: *Takes back her gem and waves her hand* They are already banished. Why did you take this in the first place?

BARD: For your own good and for the good of the Fox Cities. You already said it, these humans, they need us. You wouldn't leave your castle on my word, so I chose something you care for more than me.

LADY places her hand on his shoulder

LADY: That's not true, and I'm sorry it appeared as such. I suppose I could…help these humans find their way. Afterall, it's not a surprise that they—with their 40-hour work weeks, social media rabbit holes, and poor taste in clothing—should need the help of one such as I.

TELLER: A reconciliation! That's what that is.

LADY: Perhaps I will take that reading after all.

BARD: Now sister, how about an Old Fashioned?

LADY: I'm not old fashioned, I'm traditional.

BARD: No, no, an Old Fashioned drink. You know what, just trust me, you'll see.

Bows all around

And so, sitting on the steps of a grand staircase surrounded by the intoxicating energy of people having a good time, I tipped my glass and toasted my husband, my yellow skin slightly green in the blue lights.

When I got home at 1 AM that night—after dozens of magical folk came to tell me they wanted more, after a bar cheered me and my sister's entrance to an impromptu after party—I removed the flowy, blue dress; the long, fake eyelashes; the yellow body paint. I tucked away Delilah's fawn ears, and took one last look at the tablecloths, the party decorations, the scrolls, and treasure chests I would have to organize in the morning.

All the work of months and that day—that long, wonderful day—seeped into me. I knew it was time to stop expecting failure and stop being surprised at my own perseverance and creativity. Not that everything would work out perfectly, but rather that I should embrace myself fully, failures and successes equally examined.

That moment was the last little bit of growing up I had to do. I'm a mother and homeowner and have traveled the world, but I had been hiding a rock in my pocket. Something hard and a little mossy that I should have thrown into a still lake long ago.

The enchantment of the night had eroded the stone to nothing. Without it, I could finally spin magic.

Catwalk

Ryan Surprise

Soft, continuous static scratched Daniels' eardrums inside her helmet. The sun's glare hung on her shoulders. Her legs ebbed freely as she held to the side of the shuttle. She sighed in relief, realizing she reached the last step of the repair. She reached inside the panel with her thick gloves. She squinted her eyes as she gripped the last bolt. With effort, it gave way and tightened.

"Done," she said to herself. After closing the panel, her eyes focused on the distant abyss beyond their floating vessel. The sheer distance and scope of it caught her off guard. She roughly grasped for the railing, amending her lack of vigilance. She inhaled; her heart beat like a small, trapped bird. The static in her ears cut out.

"Engineer Daniels, are you ready for re-entry, over?" Engineer Paxton asked in his nasally voice.

Her colleague monitored the footage of the exterior camera, Paxton's pink, button nose not four inches from the screen. Daniels' small, white form floated alongside the space shuttle. She pressed the receiver inside her helmet.

"They don't pay me enough for this…coming in, over." She pumped her feet, dragging them closer to the ship against the current of anti-gravity. She closed her eyes, hearing the static still. The sun's brilliance reflected on the white shell of the ship, piercing her thin eyelids.

She moved hand over hand along the railing. She felt her hand scratch the metal and fly free from the vessel. She gasped as her eyes caught the distant stars, light-years beneath her. She pulled herself up and pressed her body against the bolted structure. She instantly reckoned her own peril in the pit of her stomach.

"Do you need assistance, over?"

Daniels breathed in as much as she could. Her vision flashed to black patches. *Breathe. Control your breathing. You can control your breathing.*

"No, I think I'm okay, over."

Her free hand stretched for the next segment of the railing. *Pull. Breathe. Pull. Breathe. Pull... Pull.* Daniels fixed her eyes on the airlock. She shuffled frantically, one hand over the other. Her feet lifted away from the ship. The cord rolling oxygen into her suit rose. She clamped onto the railing.

Stop. Stop! The cord lifted higher. She dug her shins against her suit, pulling her weight closer to the side of the ship. She caught her breath when she felt her feet vibrating against the hull.

"Daniels, are you sure you don't need assistance, over?"

"I'm fine," Daniels grumbled, "over."

She lurched forward, the last of the railing sped past her hands. She shoved her hand forward, connecting with the airlock door.

"Permission to re-enter, over."

"Standby, over."

The vacuum-pull of the emptying airlock made her muscles cling to her bones. Once her boot connected with the shuttle floor, she felt euphoric.

"Good re-entry, Daniels, over."

Paxton leaned back in his chair. Once Daniels had both feet inside, he pressed a large button on the control panel in front of him. The airlock started to close. As the stars disappeared behind Daniels, she felt a small tug in her back. She turned, glimpsing her oxygen cord in the door's path. Her last two fingers knocked the nearest section of the cord away from her.

Daniels gasped. Her lungs filled with as much oxygen as they could hold. She jumped after the door. The heavy, metal barrier could squeeze a car in half. The shoulder in her suit stretched as far as it was able. As soon as her fist clasped against the cord, she yanked it back inside.

"Daniels!" Paxton shouted in her ear. As the door slammed shut, Daniels saw the cord tranquilly float before her. Daniels breathed in, and her eyes burned at the sweet relief of assured safety.

"Daniels!" Paxton shouted over the radio; his boots crashed down the hall. Upon reaching the airlock he pounded the adjacent button on the panel. The interior door flew back. Daniels' knees buckled, she crumpled to the floor. She looked up at Paxton, joyful to see him.

"You're alright," Paxton shouted. The phrase echoed inside Daniels' helmet, giving her rest on the airlock floor. She felt her torso sag with sweat, her ribs expanding with ragged breathing. Paxton pried his colleague's helmet off, exposing Daniels' matted mop of hair. Her eyes looked petrified, blue as crystal, the irises smaller than a needle point.

Daniels looked back to the cord that sat along the floor, safely inside. She sat up and took a better look at it. The end nearest to the ship had ruptured. It must have strained against her last-ditch pull. The outer shell of the cord had bent and cracked, fraying near the air supply inside the wall.

Daniels pulled Paxton close. Her jaw jutted out, eyes level with his, so Paxton would know how serious her words were when she ordered.

"Send me back to Earth, now!"

Looking Backward

Lori O'Brian Smith

PROLOGUE

What happens to our souls when we die? It's an age-old controversy, one that brings research and debate to the ideas of reincarnation, possession, and possible communication with those departed. Dr. Ian Stevenson's book *Old Souls*, sought to verify the past lives of 2,500 children worldwide and served the specific issue that children are believed to be particularly sensitive to happenings of this nature. This is a fictional account of one such child and his journey.

The house stood in the dark shadows. What had once been a grand and inviting old Victorian, was now a sinister and foreboding presence. Emily felt like the house...old, worn, and beyond help. It was in dire need of repair. The young mother wondered if moving home with her four-year-old son Evan, was the right decision. Still, there was no other choice.

Her husband Ben had emptied their savings and, without her knowledge, had secured two additional mortgages on their home. Even her personal retirement was locked, pending litigation by their creditors.

Driving to the house, Emily held a death grip on the steering wheel. She and Evan had been left with a few personal items, a hundred bucks in the bank, and this, her childhood home. The house was her sole inheritance from her Gran, the woman who raised her after her parents died. Her memories here were happy ones–memories that didn't match the dilapidated state of the house.

The six-hour-long drive had lulled Evan into a deep sleep. Emily awakened her son and exclaimed with false gaiety, "Honey, we're home!"

By the next morning, Emily was tense with worry about bringing the house up to a suitable living condition. Threadbare carpets, a furnace with a temper, and dust so thick you could write a novel in it clouded the good points of the grand building. Emily always loved the old bowed window with the leaded glass in the parlor. As a child, it felt like a magical view of the world. The world seemed much less capable of magic now.

Sitting with her steaming coffee, her eyes welled up with tears. She couldn't help but remember Evan's question to her last night as she tucked him under the covers, "Mom, what did we do to make Dad stop loving us?" It broke her heart.

Evan was normally a rambunctious little boy. A garden of freckles across his nose, he was a man of a thousand questions. The way his mind worked fascinated Emily, but since the separation, he had become withdrawn and quiet. She had even heard him muttering to himself lately, a new trait. His inquisitiveness was alive and well, and he spent the day exploring the nooks and crannies of the house. When she asked what he was looking for, he answered, "treasure."

The old woodwork brought an air of mystery to the house. Rich, dark stains highlighted the crevices, and the young boy seemed certain he'd find a hidden door. Emily could find no harm in his exploration.

Emily discovered that the furnace was unreliable. Since her bedroom had a fireplace and as wood was abundant, she let Evan sleep in her room with her for warmth and reassurance. Truth be told, she let Evan sleep with her for her own need of loving contact. She still missed Ben and the intimacy that comes with marriage. Their physical relationship was always strong, no matter the circumstances. She had not noticed the changes in her marriage. So, for now, she let Evan stay with her.

Her education had taught Emily that children react to divorce in a variety of ways. Evan's behavior was rapidly turning into something more than restless sleep and a change in his demeanor. One day last week she heard him muttering in the kitchen, "Good Gracious, this place is in need of old-fashioned elbow grease."

Wherever did he hear that phrase? Emily wondered to herself, but she decided to put his exploration of the place to work by having him help her clean it top to bottom. It had sat unoccupied for the two years since Gran died, so every inch indeed needed a deep cleaning. She hoped that the work would make the house seem more like a home rather than just an unloved building.

Emily missed Gran more than ever now. Ben had not allowed her to take Evan to visit when Gran was dying. He felt it would be too traumatic for the boy. Gran met Evan once, when he was six months old, so she was never a part of his life. It was one of Emily's biggest regrets...not visiting more those last days. Ben hadn't bothered to attend the funeral, and missed the reading of the will because of that. She wasn't sure he understood that the house now belonged to her. A nagging feeling at the time told her to keep that information close to the chest.

Despite having a home, Emily had to find income quickly. They were broke and her credit card was maxed out. Her feelings of shame had kept her from interacting with friends. That would need to stop soon. She toyed with the idea of opening her own daycare center. She held degrees in childhood studies and elementary education, and would soon have a clean space to run it within.

Posting placement opportunities would be step one. Networking with people might offer good leads in this matter, and give her ideas of what laws and regulations were needed to open up a certified center.

The sunny farmhouse kitchen was first on the cleaning agenda. Evan stood on the counter as he took each dinnerware piece out of the cupboard and brought it to the sink for Emily to wash. One antique platter seemed to have his full attention.

He said, "I remember this platter was a wedding gift to your Grandpa and me from your Great Aunt Betty. She hand-painted it just for us. I treasure it!" Emily looked at Evan and was astonished at how he could make up such a story. It was an old platter, and was hand-painted. What troubled Emily was that he sounded like her Gran. Wouldn't a little boy rather be a superhero than an old woman? She mentally tucked the incident away, deciding that if his behavior escalated much more, she would investigate the name of a child therapist where he could vocalize his feelings. Perhaps they could see what could be done to ease his sadness over the divorce.

She could not, *would not*, involve Ben in the matter as he had made promises to Evan about visiting and calling, all not kept. What kind of man could do that to his own flesh and blood? He should not have access to Evan to hurt him again. Emily felt her blood boil when she thought of Ben's callous treatment of their son.

She was just starting to fume when Evan began singing, "Daisy, Daisy, give me your answer do. I'm half crazy all for the love of you."

She dried her hands and placed her son on the floor. Getting down to his height, she hugged him and asked, "Honey, who taught you that song? I used to hear my Gran sing it all the time."

"Gran taught me last night."

Emily was spooked and wondered what was going on. *Could the house be haunted?*

The following day, Emily pulled out the fine Italian leather checkbook, reminding her of a lifestyle that didn't exist anymore. Her body tensed when she noticed the balance in her account. The sum was under a hundred dollars. The phone and internet had to be paid because internet advertising would be crucial to daycare opportunities. Perhaps she could sell some of the antiques for quick cash. With that in mind, she mailed out the bills and with her last twenty dollars decided to treat themselves to some real lunch meat. As Gran would remind her, always "stock your larder", meaning buy milk, eggs, bread, and at least one fruit or vegetable. Always afraid of running into people Emily knew, it was time to brave the supermarket.

After grabbing a cart and corralling her son, Emily decided luck was not with her as she immediately crashed into her high school friend Libby.

"Em! You're here. Why didn't you call to tell me you were coming? And who is this fine fellow? It can't be baby Evan! He's a dead ringer for Ben." When Emily turned her head to hide her red face, Libby knew she had struck a chord. "Em, are you here alone?" Nodding her head yes and bursting into tears, Emily asked Libby to stop by after shopping so she could fill her in on the news.

Evan was impressed by the tall pyramid of apples in the fruit section, and before she could warn him, he pulled one from the middle of the group. Evan laughed to see the horror on his mother's face. "Do you remember when I was your Gran, Mom? You pulled an apple down and the whole display fell to the floor. That was so funny." The display held firm this time, thank God. Emily was thunderstruck.

How could he know that? Emily was certain she never shared that story with anyone. *Was Evan possessed? Was the house adding to the happenings?* She quickly loaded the cart with the few needed supplies and headed to the checkout counter.

Emily was dreading Libby's visit. The shame of her legal predicament, her separation, and Evan's reactions would zap what little energy she had left. At home, Evan busied himself with his animal books. Emily was glad that if occupied, his little ears wouldn't hear anything inappropriate. She jumped up when the doorbell rang.

Libby stood at the door, holding a bag of Chinese food and a bottle of wine. "I come bearing welcome home gifts." With the same enthusiasm of her teen years, she bounded into the house, straight to the kitchen and set her load down. "My God Em, it looks like I stepped back in time. I love this place. Lucky you."

"Not lucky, Lib. If I didn't have this house, I'd be out on the street with a four-year-old in tow. Ben has suddenly decided to ruin us financially and explore his freedom. Lib, I never saw it coming!"

Libby was a tall, lanky runner and felt she needed nourishment before hearing all the details. "Wait, let's get the wine poured, eat, and we can figure out your next move."

Evan came into the kitchen and hugged Libby. "Do you still like gingersnaps?"

"Why, they are still my favorite cookie, Evan. Your Mom must have told you?"

"Nope, Aunt Libby, I just remember."

The women cleaned up the kitchen and settled into comfy chairs in front of the parlor fire Emily had started. Holding back her tears, Emily ran down the last year's worth of news. She was surprised when Libby told her that Gran had confided to her that she didn't like nor trust Ben. Emily never had a clue that Gran had felt that way.

When the conversation got to Evan's strange behaviors, Libby mentioned the gingersnap comment. "You never told him that, did you? He had the same impish grin of Gran's on his face when he asked, as if he knew my reaction. What do you plan to do next?"

Emily explained the changes in Evan, his memories, and advised Libby that she would look for a child psychiatrist first thing in the morning, Evan needed to be evaluated as soon as she could afford it.

"I'll loan you whatever you need, Em, you know that. It's too important to wait. And while you're at it, find yourself a lawyer who can address the legal woes you face. Ben needs to take responsibility for the situation you are in, whether he likes it or not."

By the time Libby left, Emily couldn't have been more grateful for the happy accident of running into her at the store. For the first time in weeks, Emily felt like someone was there to rely on. She would sleep well for the first time in a long time. *You just need a plan,* she thought to herself.

The next morning, her first task was to find a good doctor for Evan. Searching on the internet, she came up with a local doctor, a woman that had many accolades from previous patients. Dr. Margaret Rice was booked out for a month, but her receptionist said she'd call back if anyone canceled so Evan could get in as early as possible.

Libby had sent a text with the name of a local lawyer, Scott Pullman. He was new to town and was hired by a prestigious firm, so there was a chance she could have better success getting an appointment. Her speculations turned out to be correct, and she was able to set up a time with him for the following Monday. She explained to the receptionist that Evan would have to accompany her. Assured that this would not pose a problem, Emily thanked them for their time, sighing deeply. She had her feet on the right path.

The feeling of accomplishment she had was a welcome spin of emotion. She'd realized she had been beating herself up for not identifying so many things, Ben's behavior for one. She felt like a loser that couldn't keep a relationship and now a mother who was failing at providing for her son. Her recent actions helped her self-esteem.

No more pity party, she thought. Emily resolved to make a new life. *These circumstances don't belong to just me. Ben played a part too.* She was beginning to feel confident that the future was in her own hands!

The following day, Emily sat at the kitchen table, writing up a list of some of the antiques that could be put up for sale. Gran had excellent taste and much of the furniture would be loved by another family. That fact made Emily feel happy to part with them.

The furniture choices made Emily think of the happy family memories that were shared around them. The phone snapped Emily out of her reverie. It was an unknown number and one she hoped was the doctor's office with good news of an opening for Evan. Her mood quickly dissipated when she said hello, and Ben's voice was the next sound she heard.

"Hey Em, surprised to hear from me? Thought you'd like an update. My attorney discovered that your Gran left you her house. It was only logical that you'd run back there. You should be hearing from them as they will need to seize the property to pay off the debts."

The fear of losing the house terrified her. Where would she and Evan live?

"I inherited this house, Ben, and your name is not on it. In case you've forgotten Evan, *your son*, needs a place to live!"

No response from Ben reiterated what kind of man Ben really was.

Emily disconnected and quickly blocked the number Ben had called from. She was relatively certain that they had lived in a state where the inheritance was hers, and hers alone. Ben had forged her signature on the mortgage docs, so her next call would be to connect with the police for an update on the fraud case. Thank God Libby had given the name of an attorney that had availability.

The phone rang again and she answered, "Ben, you are not welcome to call us anymore. Anything you have to say can be said through our attorneys." To her surprise, another voice indicated he must have dialed the wrong number, he was looking for a daycare center.

"Oh my, I'm so embarrassed, you have the right number. Please give me a chance to explain. I'm not a crazy lady, I just had been harassed by my ex and I thought you were him calling back. I do have availability to care for your child.

"Perhaps we can meet and you can tell me what you're looking for." The man hesitated, but apparently decided that it was worth a conversation. He made an appointment to bring his four-year-old son over the following day to check the place out.

The next day, Rob Kerwin and his son Casey visited. Evan and Casey took to each other instantly. Bringing Casey up to his room, Evan suggested they make a Bat Cave. Emily brought them supplies: blankets, pillows, cookies, and juice to fortify the boys.

She and Mr. Kerwin sat down in the parlor. Emily asked him what needs he had and if this job was temporary or permanent. His needs were basic, nine to five Monday through Friday. Lunch would need to be provided as well. Emily quoted him the price of twenty dollars per hour, or $500 per week if the job was a full forty hours.

He asked to look around the house, which met with his approval. It was clean and homey, with pictures drawn by little hands hanging on the refrigerator.

"How many children do you currently care for and what are your credentials?"

Emily drew in a deep breath and told him Casey would be her first, that she had an elementary teaching certificate, but had plans to pursue opening a licensed daycare. The explanation included a short, but accurate picture of her personal circumstances. The man listened carefully to her story and she felt the intenseness of his stare. He was unreadable, leaning forward with his elbows on his knees. She wondered what he was thinking.

When she asked him again the length of time for the job, he looked pensive. "My wife and I have been separated for four months. She left us and even though I am self-employed, I continue to take Casey to work with me. It looks unprofessional and he is bored silly. Another child to play with will help, and Casey too is dealing with our breakup. It doesn't look like there is much of a chance for the marriage, although I'd be lying if I didn't tell you there could be a chance. In that case, Casey's mother would be his caregiver."

Emily asked if he could ensure her of at least one month and agreed to his hope that her daycare would never service more than five children, including Evan. If more children would be added, additional certified teachers would be added and he would be made aware of her plans well in advance.

They shook hands and Mr. Kerwin called for Casey. The boys were happily playing in the fort and Casey was thrilled to hear he would be over to play with Evan the next day.

The next morning, Emily set up a chalkboard in the kitchen with the day's activities. She was going to be a professional. Their agenda included cookie baking, story time, an outdoor hike, quiet time, and an alphabet class. Lunch would be healthy but for the cookies they'd bake for dessert. Casey could take some home for his dad too.

The day went smoothly and when Casey's dad arrived, she greeted him as "Mr. Kerwin".

"Please call me Rob. You're taking care of my son and I want you to treat me as someone as approachable as I think I am!" Emily was thrilled to hear it and told him she preferred to be on a first name basis as well.

Emily had her first day of work in, money coming in to pay the bills, and Ben had left them alone since the phone call. She would have to take both boys to the law office, but she brought a way to keep them busy with activity books and crayons.

Emily and the boys arrived at the legal office, pleased to find that Mr. Pullman had toys and books and a small table set up in his office. She thanked him for his understanding and he said, "No problem, I love kids. I have custody of my two nephews. My passion for these types of cases comes from the fact that my sister died at the hands of an abusive husband. I am now the sole family for two amazing little guys and I champion cases where women can use a legal voice to set their lives back on a good path."

Emily was impressed with Scott's willingness to share his story, and it put her at ease discussing her own situation. Going over her current legal challenges took more time than Emily anticipated. Scott took copious notes and advised Emily not to have any conversations with Ben nor his legal representatives, rather, advise them to call Scott directly.

He mentioned that she should consider pursuing legal claims against Ben for the damages to her reputation and financial situation. It was decided a partner at this firm would assist her with her divorce, leaving Scott to be her primary rep for the fraud and the bankruptcy situation. To prevent Ben from seeing Evan would not be easy, or cheap. Scott asked, "Is it really in Evan's best interest to be kept from his father? Your husband sounds like a first-class jerk, but we can find ways to lessen his chances of causing emotional damage."

Emily offered, "I just want Evan to have only positive experiences with his dad. Whether or not I dislike the man is irrelevant. I don't want more emotional baggage for Evan to deal with. He already thinks he did something that made his father not love him."

"You mentioned you will be putting Evan under a doctor's care. What kinds of behavior is he showing that has you so concerned?"

Emily gave Scott the condensed version and was advised to keep track of dates and times. It would help with the litigation and help the doctor as well.

"We will pursue Ben's financial responsibility to pay for his care. As for your share of the debt to the creditors, we will not allow the cases to continue until the fraud investigation is completed. Hopefully Ben will be charged. You are correct about your house. In our state, that inheritance cannot be touched by him since his name is not on the title. His legal representatives may encourage him not to end the marriage, be prepared for that.

"Our firm will try to move the divorce through quickly, as there are no assets to speak of, just the issue of Evan. Are you looking to receive child support?"

Her reality hit her and Emily burst into tears. "I need to think, can I take some time?" Somehow, this question served to validate that her previous life was really over.

Scott said they could begin divorce proceedings without that piece of the puzzle, but not for long. Emily asked the cost for all this and Scott said she only needed to put down the retainer of $1,000. It would be a large chunk of her pay from Rob, but at least she could do that now and still have some money left over for food and bills. Life wasn't as bleak as it had been just a few weeks ago.

The weekend came and Evan spent his time in his fort or checking out the nooks and crannies of old woodwork around the house. Again, he seemed to be looking for something. He was also more quiet than usual, but hadn't exhibited any more strange behaviors. The doctor's office had called and there was an open appointment for the following week.

It would be a harrowing week for Emily. There was a hearing on the debts and the issue of her inheritance on Monday. Emily was thankful that Scott was representing her. He was empathetic to her circumstance and made the ordeal less intimidating. His self confident nature and jovial demeanor was just what the doctor ordered.

The hearing went in Emily's favor. The judge deemed that her house and all it's contents could not be breached. Scott had instinctively put his arm around Emily in court when he saw Ben glaring at her. She wouldn't make eye contact with him, and her lack of attention seemed to anger Ben. The judge advised that the court finding would be sent to all the creditors, and pushed back the hearing on those matters to a time after the investigation into the fraud was complete. Emily's body relaxed with relief.

Emily updated Scott that she would not pursue any support issues for Evan and asked the firm to move as quickly as possible with the divorce. Minimum visitation would be her preference, but for her son's sake, she decided not pursue this until after the courts decided his punishment for the fraud. It could be the matter would take care of itself if he was convicted.

Her daycare center had taken on two more children, and the income would ensure that if no money came in for child support, she could still pay her bills and maintain a meager lifestyle. There wouldn't be extra money to address any house issues, but her day-to-day expenses were no longer a worry.

The day would have been nearly perfect if she hadn't heard Ben say, "Sleeping with your attorney Em? How else would you pay him?"

Scott ushered her into his car, telling her to ignore him and said they would stop at the police station to make them aware of his harassment.

Dr. Maggie Rice sat at her desk, reviewing the questionnaire the mother had submitted. Nothing in the answers alarmed her. The exhibited behavior fell within a normal range for the young boy's circumstance. She would call in the mother first, get a feel for what was going on, including her mental state. Afterward, the doctor would spend time with Evan, assessing him while they played. Maggie had learned the best answers came when the child was in a fun, less stressful state of mind. Afterward, she would reconvene with the parent, share the assessment and a plan, if one was required.

Maggie called in Evan after speaking to a worried Emily. Doctor and child played and after some time, the doctor felt Evan shared enough for her to assess the situation. What she would share with Emily might be an unexpected bit of observation. Maggie needed to share Evan's state of mind with Emily but still open up the possibilities that more than the usual responses were happening to this family.

"Emily, that is quite the little guy you have there. Yes, he is depressed. He misses his Dad terribly, but I don't see or hear anything so upsetting that makes me think he needs medication or more than some consoling and methods he can use to come to terms with the changes."

"What about him imitating my Grandmother? How could he have known some of the things he talked about? Evan didn't know my Grandmother, she was a stranger to him."

"Fantasy in children is a natural product of going through a traumatic situation, but it *is* sometimes based on reality. Thousands of children have memories of past lives that they lived. I know this sounds hard to believe, so I am going to suggest you read up on some information. You may question it, but current thinking is that young children are unfiltered, and accept metaphysical information as if it is a natural part of life. They don't know any difference.

"Dr. Ian Stevenson, and Dr. Brian Weiss are both researchers, noted scientists that have written books on the matter. They're Ivy League trained and these books are a good place to start.

"I think I know what's going on with Evan. The good news is that memories of past lives are a way the soul can close the subject, so to speak. It seems that once the child addresses the issue, they usually stop the behavior and, with age, forget the memories entirely. Keep an open mind, Emily, and don't judge my diagnosis until you've had a chance to process the possibility. I look forward to working with Evan and helping him through this difficult time."

Emily found herself looking forward to Rob's pick up times. Casey was displaying some aggressive behaviors towards the new daycare kids. Through talking it over with Rob and sharing her techniques for dealing with them, she discovered what a kind and insightful dad he was.

She went out on a limb and asked him what they were doing for Thanksgiving.

Issuing an invitation was frightening, but his answer of, "Coming here I hope," made for an easy transition back into the dating scene.

Libby would act as her buffer. Her family was cruising over the holiday so she had availability to join the group for dinner.

Emily had feared the upcoming holidays would be sad and strange, but now she found herself eagerly anticipating them.

The holiday approached and the daycare kids made indigenous headdresses and pilgrim hats for dinner guests to wear. They drew turkeys for the windows and the old house now had an air of family and fun. Emily was able to teach the kids about different cultures, customs, and diversity at the same time. It made Emily feel she was using her teaching talents in this new profession, to the betterment of society.

Rob and Casey were excited to have Thanksgiving plans. Casey loved Aunt Em, as he called her. He and Evan were like brothers, and the new kids wouldn't be at the dinner, so he was looking forward to time alone with his buddy.

Ben was charged with fraud, but the sentencing wasn't going to happen until the fifth of January. Scott was certain that Ben would be found solely responsible once the creditors were advised. It would be a bargaining chip to use where visitation with Evan was concerned.

The divorce would be final by Christmas. Emily had purchased a gift for Evan from "his dad", just in case Ben sent nothing. He did call Evan on Thanksgiving and told him that he would try to be home by Christmas. Emily wasn't sure if she wanted him to show up or not. They had come so far, and Evan seeing Ben could just lead to more disappointment.

Evan told his mother that Gran had a special gift for Emily this Christmas but it had to wait until then. The instances of Evan and Gran conversations had faded so the comment bothered her. Dr. Rice said to let it play out and see where it led. Otherwise, Evan had been sleeping better and seemed to be his old, energetic self.

Emily made sure the daycare kids had holiday customs to celebrate. They all made ornaments while singing carols, drank hot chocolate, and everyone delighted in spending time outdoors with Rob, Scott, and his nephews. Hayrides, snowball fights, and ice skating added to the magic of the season. Both she and Evan had moments of sadness, but there were many happy moments to focus on. The new life they lived offered hope for the future and it was the best Christmas gift of all. Well, almost…

Christmas morning, Evan presented Emily with Gran's gift. An old box contained a note from Gran with many thousands of dollars. There was enough money to pay off her legal fees and get the house repaired. The note said, "I thought you may need this in the future. Make a life for you and Evan. Be happy, and know I am always with you. Love, Gran."

Gracie

Don Fahrenkrug

Love isn't won in a card game. Yes, it's a gamble. So is getting out of bed in the morning. I hadn't really thought about the baggage. I guess that's part of an entourage we think is minimal but misleading. The longer you love someone, the bigger the collection becomes. Funny in all the twists life throws, how items collecting dust become immortalized into prized possessions. Gracie's dog buddy is one of those–who is now demanding to be let outside.

I never really needed a dog. Gracie said I needed a treadmill with me showing a bit of age collecting about my waist. What a woman will do to get a dog into the house. I didn't know I needed a golden retriever but I got one now. Like everything else, I just intermittently went along with the flow. Most days begin unrehearsed, starting slowly with the sunrise. Casually I'm happy to let morning unfold, taking it in with a simple breakfast. About the time I get settled into a chair, my treadmill wants to come inside.

"Gracie, I see you left me some dishes again. You'd think after all these years of marriage I could have one day where you didn't leave me the dishes."

She has been lapse lately, leaving the household chores to me. A glimpse at the window showed a light snow falling in the bleak of winter outside. Of late, life has felt a little cloudy with a chance of weather coming. It's been a while since I felt good about anything. Life happens to all of us. Retirement into the golden years, take a deep breath and relax. Nothing to do for the rest of my life, so people told me. Biggest understatement ever spoken. I have so many things to do on our house. Projects put off for retirement, now stood demanding. The proverbial elephant in the house had a healthy appetite for eating up time.

Then it's everyone else. In my anger I blurted out, "Like, when did I become the unpaid handyman?" People are like tax collectors, everybody wants something. To their dismay and despair I've learned to say no. Gracie and I had so many plans. Why it just wouldn't do to neglect our dreams. On restless nights I succumb to the darkness. My mind retracing steps of meeting Gracie and how a room would come to life upon her entrance. She always said she needed me as I followed along in her every adventure.

I don't think anyone can tell you what love is. You have to step on it, let it squeeze up and get your toes dirty. About the time you get ready to give up on the whole notion of it, then something looks a little different. The curves you were looking at become curves of kindness. Curves of her thoughts to talk about. The way her eyes shine, and her smile curves up to greet you. It sort of works out that you think about her and dreamily want to spend time together. It'd be best to walk away from that kind of trouble but you can't. I had been walking away from love my whole life until I met Gracie. That's when I stopped walking away and embraced it. Funny how over time I have too much respect to be anything but a gentleman around her. For better or worse, she took on a handful. I got the better, she got the worse. On the surface, everything looks idyllic. Like a box of Cracker Jacks, never knowing what's inside until you open it.

With Christmas season approaching, our daughter Libby would be coming home. We needed to spruce up the house. I've let clutter collect on the dining room table and other suspect places. Wanting to make room for the tree, I gathered all things unnecessary and put them away.

Gracie always went all in for the holidays. I can remember her voice, "Charlie, carry the Christmas boxes down please," twisted around a subtle hint of demand. "While you're at it, take Thanksgiving items back upstairs." A long moment would transcend subtly, followed with a two-word reply, "Thank you."

Libby's best traits come from Gracie. I tended to be lenient. Respectful of the power balance of two girls against one guy, majority rules. Before going off to college Libby said smiling, "What mom ever saw in you I don't know. You're the kindest of fathers, but you have always been so old." I would quietly smile and be happily content with her compliment.

Some things are held private, personally intimate. I never told Libby it was Gracie who chose me. I was an introvert. A wallflower destined to be a quietly confirmed bachelor. In all truthfulness, I was hesitant. I liked women, Cupid's arrow just avoided or missed me. At my fortieth birthday, I assumed I would remain alone.

An early December snowstorm hit. Ice in a grocery store parking lot intervened. A woman screamed out while falling down. The contents of two torn paper grocery bags strewn about. I turned to the sound of some colorful cussing. Our eyes met. I smiled and helped her get up. My long snow brush reached items lost under a car. By then the wet slush covered us both. Her red cheeks of embarrassment tilted into a smile, and soon we were laughing. Not everyone sees a rainbow under black clouds. This was her way to defuse embarrassment. I was amazed that she handled this mishap while remaining composed. We talked briefly while I helped brush off her back. Through all this there was a moment of enduring kindness. As I turned to walk back to my own grocery cart she said, "Please wait, I'm Gracie, call me if you want to talk." Seemed rather abrupt. Honestly I didn't know what to think. I was left a bit shocked. She handed me a business card with her number. Later I wondered if I had been hit on by this woman named Gracie. It was something to mull about while at my own home.

Odd happenings, me getting a phone number. Me… really? After three days I nervously dialed the rotary phone. A quelled suspenseful pause followed each ring. My life dangling on a tightrope. A woman's voice answered, "Hello?"

"This is Charles, may I speak to Gracie?"

With laughter coming on the other end, "Silly Boy, this is Gracie. Wondered if you would ever call."

I really didn't know if this was the right thing for me to do. I lived a contended life. Was completely out of debt. I could come and go, free as a bird. I was middle aged old, Gracie was twenty-nine, a voice full of life. About the time our long phone conversation was ending, Gracie suggested, "Shouldn't you ask me out or something, at least see me when I'm not full of road slush?"

I was cautious, compromised with butterflies, but agreeable. Dating is a game of boundaries, and rules. Crossing bridges to who knows where. I was idly searching for my life when Gracie came along and found me.

"Mind if I call you Charlie? Seems less formal, friendlier." It was as easy as putting on a pair of socks. I was ordinary people going about unnoticed. Gracie had me feeling like I was somebody. Being different isn't wrong, I just normally remained distant.

Gracie said to me, "I'm close to you, yet you remain far away."

"I'm keeping quiet, lest I say something foolish and frighten you." This was a different kind of woman, a solemn moment when I knew there was more than what meets the eye. Gracie was someone I could be with. In this world full of people we were one small chance meeting in a parking lot. I was both afraid, and attracted. It was Gracie putting her arm in the crook of my elbow. The ice was broken. A calm washed over me. I went from being afraid to being accepted. From then on, the ship sailed a yare course. In all my life I had never felt the sense of belonging. My thoughts always drifting, unsettled. I didn't see the beginning, it was my heart that noticed the love story unfolding. Gracie had kindness overflowing. Her personality was an abrupt forward undeniable push. I, on the other hand, was the calm after the storm. In a comedy routine, I played the strait. Gracie was center stage, Mae West. Complete opposites, but what we had worked seamlessly. I never doubted that she was a capable woman. She wouldn't admit it, but she always gave me top billing. In her heart she made me feel like I was the better half. I–along with everyone else– knew better.

From our first date, my how the time flew by. After we had been together a while, our relationship remained fresh. Each day, a new beginning. When anniversaries passed it seemed we just met a week ago or so. I never tired of her company. Nor did I crowd her into living my life. It had been a long time since I was Charles. Marriage blended us into Charlie and Gracie.

Not everything is peaches and cream. Our ups and downs came in the form of children. How deeply Gracie wanted them. The heartaches of miscarriage is incomprehensible to a man. I tried to understand but realized I could only be a pillar to lean against. Someone to lend comfort. Only mothers, and the sisterhood of women can truly understand the horror, and internal blame when God takes a child from their womb. All I could do is be kind, have patience, and hope the torment in Gracie's heart would subside enough so she could forgive herself.

In time, the obstetrician would call for Gracie, asking if she was ready to try again. Everything about a lost child remains. Gently washed with tears, and quietly placed into a women's heart to never really go away. Often the memory comes back. The mother wonders what her child would look like. An intimate moment between mother and her lost child, respectfully private.

One day found us rushing to the hospital. I was there when Libby was born. Held in Gracie's arms, both of us happy with her. It was more than a change in priorities. It was another beginning to us. The family Gracie always wanted. I was demoted in status again. Once held in high esteem, each wayward wandering animal pushed me down a peg on the ladder. With Libby being born I was now an afterthought. Men quietly, succinctly pushed out of the way. I was demurely amused.

The door opened with a rush of cold air, Buddy excitedly prancing about as Libby stamped remnants of snow off her shoes. A quick look around the room and "Hello Daddy." Her hug crushed me. A greeting of emotions pouring out for both of us. "It takes my breath away coming home. You're good, Dad."

After all the surface greetings had ended, a quelled silence drifted between us. Libby's tears began, the heartfelt longing pulling us together until it became awkward. I was glad to see her, my loneliness dissipating into the warmth I had felt for Libby. Her voice sounding much like her mother's.

Libby said, "It's about Mom. It's so hard."

"I miss her too." I said. I was supposed to be strong, the adult in the room. Here I was falling apart inside. Just the two of us in our home without Gracie, both of us flooded with a lifetime of memories. It was Covid that stopped Gracie's heart and threw the rest of us under the bus. I had been in denial, many times talking to myself like Gracie was still here. Oddly in the evenings, I felt like she would walk right through the doorway and life would begin again. It was horrid to call an ambulance and watch the lights flashing down the street into the night. People put into incubators where loved ones were left out of their care. An experience too deep to fathom. Quiet funerals with no one in attendance. Churches closed, unimaginable grief to the bereaved. Such a sinister virus casting a dark shadow over humanity.

Libby and I went out to dinner, each of us avoiding the haunting details. The falling bricks tearing out pieces of our hearts. The foundation of our family crumbling. Going through a stunted conversation, Libby said, "I'm thinking of taking a semester off. I'm kind of lost, all my concentration is gone. When I try and study, I think about Mom. I'm a mess Dad, I need to be close to her, can I come home?"

How could I deny Libby? Both of us needed to heal inside. I had turned our house into Gracie's shrine. Trying to keep things the way Gracie left them. Gracie was the love that held us all together. She took all our loose threads and had woven us into a family.

I answered quietly to Libby, "That would be fine. I've been lonely myself." There never seemed to be any riffs between us before. I understood the bonds between mother and daughter, me being tails on a two-headed coin.

We made it through Christmas and in a quiet moment Libby sat at the piano. A soft melody played. Her fingers deftly touching the keys, growing into a crescendo of speed and strength, changing to a depth of anger. I listened to her frustration and powerful strokes until her pain broke the musical cadence. Libby stopped playing. The unmistakable tears streaming, pulling mascara down her cheeks. She began to wretch deeply, sobbing in a primal hurt. It was tearing her insides apart. I went to Libby and hugged her, mascara bleeding into my shirt. We needed each other more than ever.

Morning came with a soft snowfall. Buddy took up residence sleeping on Libby's bed. The light snow was Nature's wedding gown on full display, hanging frost from tree limbs in a splendid painting. Buddy was out taking a snow bath. How could anyone not like a golden retriever? Over breakfast Libby asked me if I would go to a counseling meeting with her. We all go through life, defining moments come up when you are asked to be somebody. Libby was asking for support, for me to be someone now.

"Yes, I will go with you." Much like Gracie, I would do anything for Libby.

A week later found us in chairs too uncomfortable to sit in. The waiting room antiseptically clean. A nervous pall drifting in the room. Libby and I with our lives clouded in grief, leaning over the cliff edge. The fog of bleak empty hearts hiding below.

"You can both come this way." The grief counselor led us to her office. After formalities Libby was invited to talk.

Her voice quivering in a whisper she began, "I just can't seem to function anymore. At college my mind is all over the place. I've become reclusive, careless. I don't tend to my studies. It's like I'm in a state of shock. My heart feels so empty. I wake up at night just wanting to go home. I've never felt so lost. I can't even seem to tie my shoelaces. I'm just exhausted and I don't want to get out of bed. I miss her. I miss Mom so much I hardly stop crying. My eyes just keep tearing up."

Eventually my turn came to speak, the words came slowly, my thoughts tripping over emotions. It's hard for me to open up about my life. Everything personal I've always held private, inside. "Gracie didn't leave us on her account. Her last words before they put her in the ambulance she whispered, 'I wish you love.' It remains in my mind, continually repeating over and over. The hope she carried in her heart. What she went through to have a child. Then one day, all the tears flowed down her cheeks when she welcomed Libby into the world. Gracie put reason into my life. I sometimes talk to myself like she is still here. She will always be my beacon, my home. Gracie was always the best day of my life. I miss her deeply. Everyone tells me it's time to get on with life. What life? Gracie is the only life I know. I would give the rest of my life to spend one more day with Gracie…"

It was then Libby placed her hand over mine. Her warm touch slowly gripping my hand, "Your journey's not done yet, Daddy, you still have steps to take with me."

Something in my heart opened up again. A deep sense of love poured out and opened my eyes. Gracie and I brought Libby into the world. I still had responsibilities to be the father Libby needed. My heart filled the room with love. Emotions overwhelmed us both. The heavy weight of foreboding dread had ended. Maybe we would have gotten there eventually, but this counseling opened our hearts. It was now just the two of us, and that was okay.

Libby and I walked out to the car where she stopped me, "Take me home daddy." I knew then we were going to be alright.

The next morning awoke bright with sunshine, it had been good to let the air out. As the calendar pages turned, Libby and I eventually grew to become a family again. Just like I did with her mother Gracie, I nod yes in agreement, leaving her room to grow. In Libby's own personality, from time to time I see a glimpse of her mother Gracie showing herself. In these moments I silently reserve heartfelt love…and whisper, "Thank you Gracie."

Expedition of Cul-de-sac Goodbyes

Danna Dietz

When you think about all the places you've ever called home, which places have made the most impact to put in your own personal poem?

For me, I have lived in five different locations in my 36 years on this earth, with each place testing my very own self-worth. Each house I have lived in represented diverse chapters of my being, with each residence having challenges I never thought I'd be seeing. With all that being laid out for the world to see, let me take you back to uncertain times that I wish would have allowed me to have a skeleton key.

My first home on State Street was a two-story home built in 1947 by my paternal great-grandfather and other family members, as I was told. It finally left our family forever in 2021 when it was sold.

It had characteristic eyebrow arches as you went from room to room, who knew that someday we would see it as the house of gloom. It had light blue and white seashell wallpaper all over the kitchen countertop. Sometimes I wonder whose choice this was, as today this would be considered a designer flop.

The detached garage had a wooden ladder going to the attic that was forbidden for the kids to explore, but our curiosity made it very tough for us to ignore. When my sister and I meandered into the attic and saw an old, curved wooden sled, we got excited and lost all sense of dread. We noticed a variety of other things including bird poop, feathers, and cages up there as well. My great-grandparents used to have messenger pigeons, which explained the foul smell. I found this to be really fascinating and wondered if they ever failed and fell. How interesting would that be if those birds were alive to show and tell?

On several occasions I would hear footsteps coming up the basement stairs when everyone was sleeping. It freaked me out so bad, I would head back to my bed leaping. I started to feel like this house had more secrets than I would ever find out. I was okay with this because sometimes some secrets carry a lot of unwanted clout.

Very early on I knew I was living in a house divided with my mom and dad, I knew it was not normal to see my mom that sad. My dad truly loved my sister and I (this I knew), but unfortunately, he seemed to love his adult beverages more through and through.

The neighborhood was filled with kids our age, as it was nice to get out and about and away from our dad's intoxicated rage. There were others whose parents made questionable decisions and would also fight. I remember feeling some sense of relief that I was not alone, hoping soon there would be an end to all this in sight.

I remember having to stay strong, keeping a straight face, making excuses for him and telling everyone everything was fine, not realizing how many times the police would show up due to him playing dangerously with that line. He was an intelligent, kind, fun-loving, and good-hearted man when he wasn't slamming the Blatz. We were always hoping we'd get Dr. Jekyll and not have many spats.

Four days before Christmas, my parents' divorce was finalized and all seemed like it was going to be okay. I was not sure how much longer we could all keep our emotions at bay. With the passing of my maternal grandfather on Christmas night and the passing of my paternal great-grandmother the next day, we were being pulled in so many directions that we didn't know which way to stray.

As we thought we were finally free to stay in our house and try to figure out our new normal, we were told by the family member my parents were originally renting the house from that we must leave, and it was unusually formal. We were so exhausted, stressed, and overwhelmed by already being in the fray. Regardless, that did not stop my mom from having a lot to say. I finished out my second grade school year as best as I could, I was just so ready to start over and move on, as we all should.

I knew my mom would have to switch jobs and get more help all on her own, this became the start for me to act more grown. We finally moved into our new home at the end of that cruel summer, soon enough it all became less of a bummer.

Our new home on Deerfield was quite newer and had a lot more space, we soon realized this may be our saving grace. This ranch style home had two huge maple trees in the backyard, and one in the front lawn. We loved that space so much that we would play in it from dusk until dawn. There were issues with the basement flooding more often than not, this was frustrating as the basement was ours and our friends' hang out spot.

We decided to make a special area in our backyard for our fire pit. During the summer we would host friends, and that's where we would sit. We loved playing basketball, and we were finally able to have an adjustable basketball hoop on the side of our driveway. It was not uncommon for my sister, my neighbors, and I to play a game on any given day.

The neighbors on both corners and across the street were very friendly and were always willing to lend a helping hand. We were ever so grateful to have some of the greatest neighbors in all the land.

There was not a lot to be afraid of at this home, except for the fact my sister, our friends, and I always felt we were not alone. I'm glad we were unaware of the unknown. More often than not, I did not like being alone in the house as I felt I was being looked upon, and I always had to keep the lights on. Friends would refuse to sleep in the basement after claims of them seeing a manly figure looming around by the stairs. We didn't know what to think of this as we had never seen his glares. Our mom would deny that someone passed away in the home for ten years after us asking time after time. When we moved out, she finally admitted to our suspicions on a dime.

The Deerfield ranch is where I went from a child to a lady, learning the meaning of everything on this Earth that can be shady. The ranch is where I was schooled about loss, the meaning of true friendship, and these folks having your back like a boss.

This place is where I had my first love, my high school sweetheart, my gift from up above. Everything changes when life takes you on separate trails, spreading your wings to fly like open sails.

This home is where I learned very early on how to mow the lawn and cut the weeds, doing some good deeds. This is where I learned how to properly do laundry and become a perfectionist of a normal household chore. Needless to say, it was never a bore. Winter proved to show our shoveling and balance skills, as we were trying to save on those types of bills. We would occasionally ask for help from our wonderful neighborhood handyman, Tony. He reminded me of my deceased grandfather, and I knew he wasn't a phony.

This home is where we owned our first cats, as we all learned to wear many hats. This place is where I went through some very tough times in middle school with extreme bullying and living in a constant haze, unfortunately bringing on some dark days. Thankfully, amazing family and a neighbor's support pulled me from this unpredictable phase.

I was full of bittersweet emotion knowing we were leaving this all behind the fall I started my freshman year of college. At the same time, I felt ever so grateful for having been blessed with all this life knowledge.

Our twin dominium on Blake's was a home my family and I got to help design as much as we could foresee, from the half-finished basement, to the color and pattern of the countertops, to where our new gas fireplace would be. First time we would ever have a fireplace inside to enjoy in the wrath of the winter's cold. It really could make the holidays that much more cozier and bold. It was amazing to see it all come to fruition in real time, thanks to our hard work and letting our imagination climb.

Living at home with family in a new environment while starting college was quite the wakeup call. It was a dissimilar trajectory as we had a hard time adjusting to someone living on the other side of the wall. It helped to meet our neighbors and know that they all seemed pretty nice, especially a few of the older ladies who had a lot of spice. One of my mom's best friends built a home a few doors down. Being this close was great, as we loved having them around.

Our home was one of the first built on the cul-de-sac across the street from the baseball diamonds and soccer fields. It was neat to see the neighborhood start to grow as we became each other's shields. We had a large front yard but smaller in the back; the flower garden and porch swing were quaint as the backyard view did not lack. The beautiful open field beyond our flower garden was filled with all kinds of wildlife we never expected. This was such a great place to read, write, and let your thoughts be reflected.

We knew most of the folks on our little road and most were willing to help out if we needed it, this boded well for us as we all would see fit. We helped a few of our elderly neighbors with yard work and if they fell, we were often on high alert with some, making sure we always had our cell.

My sister and I having our own little sleeping and living space in the basement was something we were grateful for, and was well needed. At that time, the expectations of our freedoms were exceeded. The basement became my study sanctuary and place to chill, I had occasional parties with family and friends that were quite the thrill. We had more independence in this home as well as more responsibility, as any adult should. We were young, wise, and trying to become less misunderstood.

College at UW-Fox Valley was exciting, fun, interesting, and not too far away from where I laid my head at night. I was excited to get my career in psychology started, with my end-game in sight. During this time, I fell in love with a guy I met through a best friend. I felt I was on cloud nine and that my mind wouldn't bend. He got a dog that I ended up taking care of as I felt like he was becoming my pup too, I finally felt like I had what I was working and waiting for as if he knew. I got a new job and was doing better in school, hoping and praying I wasn't looking like a fool.

Over two and a half years together we felt it was the right time for us to look at a house of our own, here we go about to take out another loan. At that age, we were still trying to figure out who we were and what we wanted in our journey through life. We started having complications and at that point, I had a feeling I may never become his wife. A week before we were going to move into our new home and become happy as can be, he came over to my house and broke it off with me. This crushed me in a way I never knew I could feel, I became so overcome with emotion and failure that I could hardly deal.

As time went on, I graduated with my Associates in Liberal Arts and Science, I had so much more confidence and self-reliance. I met so many intelligent people that I become so thankful for, I was ready for the adventure to a bigger campus at UW-Oshkosh as I'd been yearning for more. This college was much more diverse and kept my mind wanting to learn. I was so ready for success because dammit, it was undeniably my turn!

I faced many unforeseen turns and twists and ups and downs, I was more than hoping I was not going to be over my head and beginning to drown. The professors, students, classes, and college culture were fascinating as far as the campus could see; I was ready to dive in and be involved with whatever made me feel free.

During this era, I reconnected with my first love who had over time evolved into a good friend at the same college. We had no idea what to expect from each other aside from the fact we were there to gain more knowledge. We genuinely enjoyed each other's company and talked about starting to date again, as for a third time I did not want to bid him a farewell. One night out during some live music, I knew I'd lost him to another woman who had him under her spell. It killed me once the realization became a reality and took me a while to make peace with this as I was trying not to dwell. I could not blame him though, as I knew this woman was pretty damn swell.

After I knew I lost him forever, I started hanging out with someone I met when we were younger years back. We hit it off immediately, which got us some flack. We fell in love hard and fast; we were confident we were going to last.

Little by little the lies and insecurities came into light. We started becoming people we feared, and that's when we would fight. I was seeing less effort go into work, friends, and family, and putting more effort into making a life with someone who was not on my level, as I started to see my passion for school go south like the devil.

The basement became my hiding place more than ever. My gut kept telling me my feelings for him I needed to sever. When that relationship ended, I got a new job at a major retail company close by. I started attending a new college, and excelled in my new career change, which put me at an all-time high.

Classes were much more intense than I had ever predicted for a program like that. My bedroom became my study hall oasis with just me, caffeine, snacks, and the cat. With my second Associate's degree, I knew student loans were going to be pouring in with the months to come. I got a second job bartending, and that's when I met the man, who again, could make my heart beat like a drum.

I began to spend more time away from my safe haven to be able to be more available for him and his kids' lives. Little did I know, we'd be living in a duplex three short months later talking about school sports and schedules, giving each other high fives.

The Plainfield duplex was a two-bedroom, one bath, one story place that was quite spacious and cute. We were blessed to share the other side with two wonderful people who were quite a hoot. It was conveniently down the road from a well-known bar. This was conducive, as we could walk and not worry about having to drive our car. It was my first time away from my family and quite a new quest. I was nervous and overwhelmed, and hoping it would work out for the best.

I fell in love with his kids and I felt I had a legitimate responsibility to be a good role model and be present in every respect, this was becoming everything my heart was hoping to expect. It was very short lived as we realized this was not going to work. I moved back home with my sister and my mom, and couldn't believe how much he was a jerk.

Coming back home to live with my sister and mom was unexpected due to financially having no other choice. I had to swallow my pride and work hard again to find my voice. This home taught me a thing or two about autonomy and how unpredictable this world can be; I needed to fall before I could rise, learning nothing in this life is a guarantee.

I learned that I truly enjoyed liberty on my own. I now could not wait to lay my roots down and carve my independence in stone.

Three years later, I finally made the jump and got my very own apartment with quite the space. I was blessed for friends and family to help me move as they are my saving grace. I have a one-car detached garage, and a nice-sized patio to relax in the back. Really not too shabby even with things that lack. Having two walk-in closets is amazing for storage and clothing, with all this capacity, I should not be loathing.

I'm impressed by my very own exuberant interior decorating making my place quite quaint, too bad I am not able to make it more my own as I am not able to use any type of paint.

We have one washer and dryer in the hallway of our building for all the tenants to share. I cannot tell you how much this is an annoying struggle as it's something we all duel to declare.

Sadly, we cannot have any pets with the exception of a rare few. So I figured a fish would be a great view. I miss not being able to have a cuddly, purring furball greeting me at the door and laying on my lap. Hopefully one day soon, I'll get my loving pet and we can take a long cat-nap.

The usual noises from other tenants, doors slamming, people stomping and being loud as can be; it's very taxing to everyone, not just me. I really hope I don't have to deal with this constant stressor too much longer every day and night because it's igniting my fight or flight.

I've been blessed with some pretty great neighbors throughout the years. And of course there have been a few who are my dreaded lively fears. I worked relentlessly to make this unknown residence comfortable and welcoming for myself and the folks I love most. There's only been several times over the years I've been able to share this place with a toast.

It has been overwhelming and extremely trying more often than I'd like, but I just use this all as a learning curve instead of taking a hike. I've dated here and there, but only once have I been in love with a man who was leaving for a job that I considered dropping my entire established life to move across the country with. I have lost family members and friends to all sorts of illnesses, and just simply growing apart and admitting pleading the fifth.

I signed a one-year lease and decided I will move after that time is over. Little did I know it wasn't that simple, and I was not as lucky as a four-leaf clover. I've been here longer than I planned and it could be worse. I just count my blessings and pray I don't fall under some apartment curse. We will see what escapades the future fairy continues to bring; someone please manifest somewhere I can be happier and not controlled like a puppet on a string.

As you sit there and read this with your choice of beverage in hand, how many times can you recall having left for somewhere new that was planned? When you take a stroll through the tough, yet nostalgic past, what stands out most to you that will make your memories last? Every house can become a home with tenderness, love and care. Just be sure to choose wisely, as it's something you should be able to bear.

We never know how much strength we emit until being strong is the only choice we must make; we need to learn to let our instincts guide us and sometimes be okay with what's about to be at stake.

A new residence and its local community have a way of taking us on unforeseen adventures and guiding us to a new frontier. It is indeed a surprising learning process, which can make us become our very own pioneer. We all have a story of where we came from and where we plan on going, just remember it should be up to you to choose which way the river is flowing.

All I Need to Know

Eric Reuter

There were many things I had learned during my life that I'd never fully understood. Religion, politics…math; these were just a few things I felt would never help me. As I closed my eyes, I reflected on everything I had learned.

When I was born, everything was new to me. Every sight and sound excited me. Shapes and colors, soft and rough, learning to crawl and exploring my surroundings. I learned what gave me joy and which things I despised. This was my entire world. At that moment, I figured this would be all I needed to know.

As I grew and I learned how to walk, my world expanded exponentially. I learned how to run and to repeat words. I imitated my parents and their smiles. This, I felt, was all I needed to know.

As I grew older, the scope of my knowledge continued to expand. I experienced the challenges of reading and writing. Trying to memorize proper sentence structures made my head spin. I don't know how many times my hand would cramp up trying to keep every letter perfectly within the dotted lines of the practice paper.

My parents taught me the concept of right and wrong as well as proper manners and etiquette. Most of these lessons filled me with boredom and irritation. Surely, I felt, that after learning all of this, I would know everything that I needed to know.

Once I became an adolescent, school became my new frontier. Teachers filled my head with all of the knowledge they claimed I would need to know to be successful in life. While they broadened my education, there was another jungle that had to be navigated: the society of my peers. Deciding which groups were right for me, making new friends, and choosing whether to go with whatever new "it" thing was at that moment. Though my head spun trying to keep everything straight I believed, after learning all of this, then that would be all I needed to know.

As time went by, my mindset had broadened further. I was introduced to new races, cultures, and creeds. I learned to be open and accepting of all. I've gone through many hardships and heartbreaks until I found that special someone to share the rest of my life with.

I found myself navigating yet another frontier. Finding a perfect balance of being a responsible employee, a devoted spouse, and a loving parent. I hope I had learned all I needed to know to teach them all they needed to know.

As the years went by, I took things easier. After retirement and the occasional trip with my spouse, I thought my life would be filled with nothing but mundane repetitiveness. Thankfully I was blessed with many grandchildren to fill my days with laughter and joy. I can teach them all that I know, like how to have fun without the aid of electronics. Seeing the smiles on their faces makes me hope that they too will learn all that they need to know.

I have grown old and frail. Every day seems to be a struggle to do simple tasks like getting up or walking to the bathroom. My body creaks and aches with the slightest of movements. I can tell my time on this plane of existence is almost at an end. Friends and family have all come to say their final goodbyes. As I lie here, I wonder, "Is this it? Have I learned all that I needed to know?" But then I realize that, through my faith, there is one more frontier that awaits me once I leave this mortal world. I smiled and closed my eyes as I finally understood. In the great mystery of life, there is no such thing as all you need to know.

An Open Invitation

Don Fahrenkrug

Nothing is known about the future. The choices to be made. A thin line exists between adolescence and the crossing into adulthood. I was at the cusp of maturity, finding an unknown path touching the fabric of love. With lack of experience I would be tested in moments that defined character and friendships. The summer months were about to begin.

The late sunset languished amid an orange-rouge skyline. My toes stirring the placid surface of Lake Poygan. The warmth of spring found me at the end of the dock contemplating. At nineteen I had escaped home into the phrase of finding my life.

"Your younger brother needs your bed," my mother had said, succinctly abrupt. I was the sixth of ten children. The moment had arrived to grow up.

I milled about a life sharing rent with two others. I tired of the stealing of food, beer going missing, the petty arguments over nothing. A cottage across the lake came up for sale. Solitude has its price, I moved. Rustic was an understatement. All the comforts of an outhouse, running water from an artesian well, and electricity. A far cry from Frank Lloyd Wright designs, but I was living on the steps of nature.

Competitiveness stirred inside. I was swept into the arena of hydroplane racing. It combined a mechanical aspect with the thrill of adrenaline, and the element of water. Imagine a boat, eleven-feet six-inches long traveling a few heartbeats past ninety mph. Racing chine to chine, twelve boats abreast going full throttle into a first turn wide enough for three boats. Who breaks first, who pushes into the lead? Like wild horses running with the wind. A selfishness develops into fearlessness. The will to win is a speed rush flooding into blood veins. Everything captured into a fleeting moment of suspense.

The summer racing season raised money for non-profit organizations. Burlington, WI was the first boat race of the year held on Memorial Day weekend. I would pit my boat next to Steve, Skip, and Joe. Skip and I raced E-modified hydro. Steve and Joe raced other classes. We shared holding boats until the coarse judge would call out the boats. Race days were filled with lots of waiting time with many classes of boats to run. We had a boom box playing The Beach Boys. It was an earlier time of cassette players.

Joe's brother Mike drove from Milwaukee, bringing along Audrey. After introductions, she took one of the lawn chairs making herself comfortable. Mike disappeared into the vast crowd. Audrey was a noticeable girl. Her brunet hair bobbed at the top of her neckline, pulled back from her face, accentuating her eyes. Her smile was a natural fit. It was a welcome warm day, one to be remembered.

Mostly small talk in the air filled with indifference, yet somehow the subjects between Audrey and I had changed. In a deeper sense, we were flirting. Audrey asked personal questions delving into who I was. I felt honestly open. An inner revelation awakened to just be myself. I had always been a loner in life. The sixth child of ten, I mostly looked to escape people.

In a way, solitude brought blissful peace. I lacked some of the social skills to interact with women while remaining at ease. Unpolished about relationships, but then I wasn't in one. As the day drifted on with the few clouds above, the presence of Audrey was comfortable. There were no filters between us.

As the evening fell away, before Audrey and Mike left, she placed her hand on my shoulder and said, "Thank you, I had a lot of fun today."

Later that night I thought about words spoken between us. I thought about a girl. I thought beyond myself, of friendship, kindness, and towards a much bigger picture of life. Then I saw her walking away with Mike. Some thoughts I'd like to forget, but they seemed inescapable. Before the summer was over, I would learn much about enduring the limits of friendship, and the cruelty residing within us.

A Beautiful Girl

vague encounters
of shapes and colors,
unknowns explicitly hidden.

a kind heart,
thoughtful mind,
personality with a smile.

intangible character traits,
all the threads become woven
into someone beautiful.

Skip, Joe, Steve, and I would spend spring days fishing walleyes on the Wolf

River. Later would come casting for northern pike with Little Cleo's and drifting June bug spinners for walleyes. A local tavern in Boom Bay had a juke box, and served cheeseburgers. It was a good place to congregate, playing pool being the biggest draw. We burned off energy playing basketball on a blacktop court outside of our house. Between working and loitering away the summer days, life seemed rather idyllic. It is quite ironic on how much the underaged girls looked for our attentions. We all understood the trouble and implications involved. Steering ourselves away from the slang monicker of jailbait.

We had boat races in Menasha, Hahn-a-Lula, Fort Atkinson, and Manawa. When we went to race in Oshkosh, Mike showed up with Audrey. Her and I remained like best friends. An inadvertent complexity developed between us. When a girl looks at you with interest, you don't need to say anything, unspoken words tell a deeper story between eye contacts. Beyond an educated doubt I was interested, you could say deeply smitten. I wasn't alone. There was a subtle chemistry growing between us. In two days of boat racing Mike's insistence of avoiding Audrey showed. She spent most of her time in one of my folding lawn chairs. It became apparent how Mike and Audrey lacked a basic friendship toward each other. Maybe it was his need to hang out with his brother Joe, or a want to fit in with the camaraderie of racers. At that moment, Audrey was Mike's arm candy, left behind as an afterthought. As of yet it hadn't occurred to me that girls too were searching for a place to fit in. Someplace where they would feel welcomed among friends.

After races end and crowds disperse, cleanup begins. Race buoys needed to be pulled, patrol boats trailered, official tents taken down. Race boats are stripped of their motors, stainless steel propellers packed protectively away, tools packed up. I would end up smelling of gasoline, smeared with grease, and looking like a wet dog with water squishing in my tennis shoes. I liked boat racing. Somewhere in the chaos of packing and goodbyes I let the words, "I'll see you again," slip from my lips. Intentional or not Audrey had a look of seriousness. One that was unavoidable, which quickly turned into a smile of uncertainty. She and Mike left shortly after. I stood silent with emotions stirring deep within my thoughts. I was living in a house of cards standing inside a room with Mike and Audrey strangely feeling like I didn't belong. The deep consequences of my actions were looming over all of us. Heavy clouds gathering in storm not quite ready to empty themselves in a deluge.

Fremont was the racing destination the next weekend. In some ways a dangerous course, the way the docks from the two bars downtown extended out into the river making a dog leg turn on the strait-away. The judges split our race into two groups of six boats, with eight boats in the final.

I was surprised when coming to shore that Mike and Audrey had come to Fremont. Joe was scrounging parts for a blown motor and didn't race. I took my turn in the patrol boats, then stepped up to race in eleven hundred hydroplane. Sometimes they would be short of entries, and it was another boat ride. I didn't say much to Audrey, not after she told me she had moved in with Mike. I felt like a little boy in a suit sized much too big holding a long stemmed red rose with no one to give it to.

Anyway, the boats were scattered in town without a park to stage them in. It would be hard to walk away with so many spectators in and around the race boats. An idiot of a spectator left a half full can of beer on the hull of my boat, leaving a white ring in the blue paint. Sometimes you just take a deep breath, life happens.

We had a free weekend coming, early August and the sweetcorn was in. I decided to throw a cookout party. I told Skip, Joe, and Steve bring anyone you want. Somewhere around ten people came on Saturday afternoon, Joe came by boat across the lake with Mike and Audrey. It was an afternoon break from life. We all needed to unwind on a lazy summer day where just chilling out was welcomed. Alcohol and sun mixed together can make some giddy. Too much can bring out traits people most likely want to hide. When those faces show themselves, a stark reality conflicts with what's right and wrong. Anger stews in the pot only so long before it spills out.

As the afternoon reached long into evening, the party ran its course. I had food to put away and dishes to carry into the cottage. Audrey also carried some into the kitchen where we shared some small talk. It was brief, maybe longer than I thought. Perceived innocence is deceiving. Alcohol and jealousy are a bad combination.

Mike and Joe got into an argument outside, ensued with a shoving match. That about ended the party. Joe, Mike, and Audrey boated back across the lake. The party cleared out. I was eventually alone in my thoughts contemplating circumstances. Darkness was riding a cool breeze as my toes pushed into the sand. I walked to the end of the dock then swam out peacefully. Water always feels good. Cool enough to feel refreshing, invigorating. In the confines of the bay a stillness prevailed. Out on the lake was turbulence, broken occasionally by whitecaps. I didn't suspect anything but a cool night with the sound of crickets. If the wind picks up, waves washing ashore would be music. In the wash of waves lives a relaxing song that soothes stress away. In solitude I had learned to like the sounds of nature. Such a peaceful easing of my mind.

Beating Hearts

softest white flower petals,

deftly searching, lingering,

whispering about emotions,

stirred delicately,

how deeply this love

touches my heart.

to mislead;

in anyway harm,

mentally, or physically hurt,

would be unjust,

love cannot be taken,

only given from the heart.

both uplifting and exhausting,

filled with futile delusions,

and captivating rewards,

like raindrops washing windowpanes,

a somewhat distorted view,

into a future yet undetermined.

It was well after nine o'clock when a boat pulled up to the dock. I had heard the motor coming into the shore. In the boat was Audrey. I thought, how foolish to cross the lake alone at night when she didn't know it. Mascara smeared on her face told a different story.

Softly she asked of me, "Do you have any ice?" Her left cheek sported a deep red welt. What had been a tense feeling moments ago, became calmly subdued. Kindness in our voices, both of us listening to one another.

"Mike hit me. He grabbed my arms, told me I was nothing but trash." Her words sunk in deep. The pain made her voice waver. An untold fear showed in her eyes. That she found the cottage at all was a relief. The shoreline looks totally different after dark.

Control

a heart that controls

another's heart,

is no heart at all,

just another thief,

stealing someone else's

dreams.

Her clothes were all wet. I asked, "Would you like some dry stuff to wear?"

I led her inside the cabin and handed her a towel, sweatpants, and an oversized tee shirt. She went into the bedroom to change. It was a while before she came out again. I had warmed some water on the stovetop. She washed her face in the kitchen sink. Standing all disheveled and without makeup, I was looking at a different kind of beautiful.

Quietly she said, "Thank you. I was hoping you were home. Really I didn't know where I was going, I just had to leave. Then I found myself coming here." At that moment I had felt a growing empathy, something in my heart reached for Audrey. Confused in my own emotions, yet wanting to protect her. A woman should never be hit, not ever, period.

"His anger just exploded." She said, "I thought I could change him…change him to be someone I wanted. I didn't ask to be punished!"

I didn't need an explanation, but Audrey continued on. Maybe talking more to herself than to me. She could have been in shock, stunned by the suddenness of the events happening.

"I'm sorry I barged in on you." Standing up pacing about nervously, she said in a soft whisper, "I have never really felt loved."

Her statement hit me hard. A horrible knife cut where I couldn't stop the bleeding. I wanted to hug her, hold her, but the moment escaped me. I was inept. Wishing to pour myself forward and lean into her. Instead I failed her. Trembling inside with my own fears. I had never told anyone that I loved them. I was unprepared to be who she needed.

Trying to defuse a rising tense moment, and wade through her last statement, I sat at the kitchen table, telling her, "Everything will be okay, take a deep breath, and relax."

"Are you that dense?" her voice rose. "I'm living with a guy who just hit me! Wake up, Stupid."

I quietly left that hanging like a kite flying over my head. I would rather walk away than say something I couldn't take back. Her anger with Mike spilled out between us. I was stepping into deep mud, her mud. All the anguish oozing between her toes, knee deep in a cesspool of problems called life. I wanted to offer an olive branch. An escalating drama playing itself out in the confines of the cabin. In a room with no winners, we both grasped at straws.

It took courage for her to open up to me. It's emotionally heartfelt when someone lets you inside. I hadn't experienced this type of intimacy before with a friend, much less a woman. Something was melting inside me. For the first time I was seeing more than curves and a smile. I lost the selfish attitude of adolescence. Understanding her circumstances, becoming the friend she reached out too. A herd of elephants could have ran through the room, it would not have mattered, I was the someone who Audrey came to in the night.

I guess I was choking inside. So many stirring emotions. For a long while

I was stupefied, then I said, "Today you had a really bad day. Tomorrow you can sort through your options, then decide what to do. This is just one day, that's all it is, just one day."

Audrey was sifting through a caldron of thoughts. Distant, quiet, unsettled, whispering quietly, when she said, "I'm just so tired of it all." In that moment, she looked defeated.

What started out as an arm around her shoulder, turned into an emotional hug. Two people in the middle of a bridge, life colliding us together. The brevity of her situation stained the space between us. It was approaching eleven o'clock and I said, "It's too rough to cross the lake tonight. If you want, I can drive you around the lake."

She said, "I'd rather not deal with anything more tonight."

"If you want, you can sleep on my bed. I'll sleep on the sofa."

She said, "I can't take your bed."

"Yes, you can." She walked into the bedroom, soon enough it was quiet so that the night sounds came in through the open windows. Waves were spending their anger on the shoreline. Leaves rustling in the wind. The crickets serenaded in response to night's darkness.

With sleep some distance away I heard Audrey's voice, "Are you still awake?"

"Yup, I'm awake." I answered.

She was in the doorway, "Want some company?"

"Busy day, wasn't it?" I said.

"That's an understatement." Sitting on the sofa next to me, the room dark but for moonlight creeping in she asked, "Is there anything between us?"

The weight of her question smothered me. I was afraid to tell her that I'd never been with a girl before. I didn't understand a woman's capacity for kindness. Thinking on that I answered, "I was off guard when you asked me,

'Can you sing?' I liked the challenge and all, but you caught me flat footed. That was at the first boat race, in Burlington."

Audrey said, "You didn't answer my question."

"I noticed you when you first arrived, straw hat, sunglasses, and sandals."

She coaxed me on, "You can do better than that."

"Okay, you're the first girl to sit in my lawn chair while I worked on my race boat. I hadn't really thought about being alone. After Burlington, I thought about you."

As if pulling my teeth she asked, "How much?"

"I had moments where I felt so distant, alone. I feel nervous now, yet very close to you."

"You're embarrassed." She said, "I can tell it in your voice, that's kinda cute." There were long pauses between questions and answers, both of us stepping on eggshells. Both unsure of the path before us. We talked about life, childhoods, likes and dislikes, who we were inside. Time has a way of running away when you need it most. We never noticed the clock ticking, or the hands passing three o'clock in the morning.

Audrey asked, "Something changed after Fremont, you changed. You got all serious looking and didn't talk freely anymore. What happened to you?"

It was pulling my heart out. How do you tell someone you're falling for them, when she's someone else's girlfriend? When you're just a wallflower, a bystander behind another guy?

"You said you moved in with Mike." My words fell with such finality as I whispered them out. It was such a deep line drawn in the sand. It took a moment for me to cross. "I didn't know how to react. I had thoughts about us. When I heard you moved in with Mike everything crumbled inside me." My voice but a trembling whisper, emotions pouring out of me, I became pensive, searching inside for the right answers.

Audrey calmly, quietly said, "I didn't know you cared that much about me."

Abruptly I stood up, looking away, seething inside, beside myself, gathering before I spoke. Turning towards her I said, "Audrey I have never had a girlfriend. Just a few dates with the wrong girls. Me, them, I don't know, it just didn't matter. It takes me a long time to open up to someone. I was never intended to be a one night stand. Audrey, you matter to me."

Quietly the room settled down. I think we were both sorting through the words said. Tensions rose and fell, then rose again. Up to our necks in a pall of emotions pent up inside. With all of our thoughts now spilled out on the table, and it being late, Audrey and I stood up. She put her arms around me and squeezed the wind out of me in a hug. The kind you wish would never end.

So many thoughts drowning me as she said, "You're a really nice guy." She turned away, I watched her shadow go through the bedroom door. Saw the door close. I stood there, the little boy in the room, in the oversized suit, holding the long stemmed red rose as the world collapsed around me.

When morning came, the wind had subsided. The lake shimmered as the pink sky unfolded. I was sitting on the porch when Skip, Joe, and Mike pulled up to the dock in a boat. It all seemed surreal. The three of them clomping on the dock boards. The boat Audrey had taken tied to the dock. I sat on the porch. Audrey was still sleeping. The jury was in. They had found me guilty. Naturally it was all my fault. The three of them peering at me like they would a fox in the hen house. Like most of last night, again I was contemplating circumstances. The hell with those clowns. Audrey had gotten up still wearing my tee shirt and sweatpants. She came to the cottage door.

Mike said, "We figured you would be here. Get your stuff."

I asked Audrey, "Do you want me to give you a ride home or anything?"

She said, "No." Then went back inside the cottage and grabbed her clothes.

The emotions of last night were quietly subtle. A chill had left fingerprints between Audrey and I. Stepping out on the dock, I watched them get into the two boats. Audrey looked at me the whole time as the boats moved away. It was a forlorn foreboding look, like those you see at a funeral or something distressful. Hindsight tells me I should have held her, pleaded with her not to go. I didn't know how to explain love. After she said no, part of me went empty inside. I was in free fall waiting for the ground to come up and crush me.

This was the last time I would ever see Audrey. I heard she called her father to help her move away from Mike. Joe told me I was the reason Mike got rid of her. People often come to conclusions, seeing evils to soil reputations. Innocence is often found guilty without evidence. When the bag was torn open, all the ugliness spilled out. I couldn't ignore what happened to Audrey. Character and maturity had finally caught up to a little boy's adolescence. Realities of life being a harsh teacher. The guys I thought to be friends came up a little shallow. Audrey gave me a summer where I grew up. I felt deeply in my heart a love beyond my dreams. It was the first time I really understood beauty. I'd like to think she needed to distance herself from everything Mike. I was unavoidable collateral damage.

It's midway into September, a month has passed since Audrey came across the lake. Love has changed me. I look the same, but everything is different inside. I'm sitting at the end of the dock. The yellow willow leaves are falling on the water's surface. Like small lifeboats they drop into the water and drift away. My mind contemplating back to a summer day in Burlington when a girl asked me to sing. Audrey touched my heart deeper than I knew. When the wind carries the water into shore, and waves wash back and forth in the presence of my emotions, I feel a closeness to a girl with auburn colored hair, and a curving smile who for some reason needed me. It was my awakening to the powerful feelings of love. I would question those I thought were friends and look at women much differently. Somewhere out there exists a powerful love, and a heartfelt sense of belonging. My life's path has just begun…

Audrey

released you, so you could fly,

yet you remain, to flutter in my mind,

like a butterfly in the wind, dancing,

tormenting my thoughts, then gone once again,

returning sometimes, when I need you most…

Permafrost

Elizabeth Westenberger

The breeze bites at the uncovered part of my face. Snow seeps between the layers of my cloak. It comes undone, dark red against the expanse of white and powder blue. I pull at it, trying to clasp it together, but echoes of the cracking ice beneath me take precedence.

I let the cloak fly behind me and look across the ice to find shallow lines growing bigger, taking over the lake. I've felt this fear before and I can feel it now. Descending below, surrounded by gray, the cold picking and prodding at me until there is nothing warm left inside or out, and I disappear. The sharp wind throws me from my flashback. That's when I realize there's no one to help me this time. I'm on my own.

My only company are the projectiles of ice shooting through the pink sky, coming straight at me. I manage to dodge most of them, clutching the frozen egg to my chest, but one of the spikes pins my open cloak to the splitting floor. Spiderwebs dance across the frozen water, but I manage to wrestle out of the fabric's grip before the ice shatters. It still takes too long. Long enough for the source of the barbs to catch up. The arachnid's long, piercing legs skitter over the lake in a morbid ballet.

I don't have long to make a decision. Judging from its stark, white fur, it must be the ice spider of Acrimel. If I don't hurry, its spikes could land, poisoning me in the process. A portal could help me get out alive, but the last dimension I traveled to, well, I don't want to go back. Not yet, not when I'm so close. A shadow looms over me. It's getting closer, going in for the kill. But the shadows give me an idea.

The icy egg chills through the remainder of my clothes. I hug it tighter with one hand and use the other to find, where is it? There, behind the knife attached to my belt. A vial, the contents a swirl of black in separate shades. Without thought, I hurl it over my shoulder and pick up speed, hoping it will be enough.

I hear a squeal and chance a look back. Shadows slink and rise around the spider's legs. I will never know the fullness of how this world works but something tugs in me. Guilt maybe? The darkness pulls the creature down until it's nothing but a silhouette on the surface of the lake. The spider won't make it after March, soaking into the lake until it disintegrates into nothing.

A pang of guilt shoots through me, but I shake myself back to the present and move on, not wanting to stay on this stupid ice longer than I need to. I've obtained the last ingredient, and in this business, it's best not to linger.

The warm light calls to me as I stagger through the doorway. It's night but the halls are busy with red, black, and white cloaks, their shoes making a clacking on the black stones. Other residents are finishing the day's project. Some read while they walk. Some strut along, levitating candles drifting behind. The tiny lights cast shadows onto the walls.

The scent of chocolate, sage, and cleaning oil tempts me toward the kitchen but I think better of it. The egg is getting warmer by the minute and I don't need it hatching in here. I'm already on thin ice with the housemaster.

It's not until I turn to go down the dark stairwell that I can fully relax. Most people are out working on their own projects and rent isn't due for another week. There's no reason for me to go back upstairs. I can finally work in peace.

Ouro meets me as soon as I open the door to my room. I give her a quick pat, taking comfort in the glossiness of her red and white scales as she slithers around my legs lovingly. I want to stay longer but I've been waiting years for this opportunity. Now that I finally have everything there's no point wasting any more time.

"Don't worry, sweetie, I'll be back soon. Then, when I get her back, we'll go for walks again, just like we used to. I promise."

Running to the other side of the room, I gather the necessary ingredients. To the ice egg I add a bottle of pure shadow from the shadow realm, a little bit of gold extract, petals from an astra flower, and–

Where is it? It's supposed to be here. I've been gone for a week and milk snakes don't like the taste of mercury, so my precious Ouro wouldn't have taken it. No one would take a chance on stealing from me. Unless someone discovered what I'm up to, but if they wanted to steal my discovery and take it for themselves, wouldn't they take everything?

It dawns on me then. Mentally scolding myself for not realizing sooner, I waste no time. My door cracks against the brick wall, echoing through the hall. The deeper I go, the darker it gets until only a few gaslights cast shadows over the doors. I approach the last one on the right and knock. No reply. Only a sharp, ringing sound behind the metal hinges. I should wait, a gentleman doesn't barge into doors, it isn't polite, but she started it.

As the door opens, screeching sounds advance, coming straight for me. Pressing forward despite the annoyance, I approach the figure hunched over a giant stone wheel.

"Okay, give it back."

"Oh, hey, Julius. It's nice to see you too. Fine evening, isn't it?" Sora says, not looking up once from the grindstone, ignoring the popping sparks.

"It would be better if you didn't keep taking my things."

She doesn't stop tinkering. The sound of metal against stone piques my annoyance with every second. Why would she do this? Doesn't she know how much this means to me?

Right when I feel like I can't stand the noise any longer, she stops, eyes still on her new creation. "Why do you think I would do such a thing? And here I thought we were friends."

"C'mon, Sora, who else would it be? I know you don't like what I do."

I have her full attention now. Her hands shake as the sparks stop. I try to stop mine from doing the same but fail. So, I put them in my pockets instead.

"It's wrong. Do you really think Hettie would want this?" Sora asks.

The use of her name stings. She may as well have used one of her weapons on me. I manage to return my breathing to normal and ignore the gripping feeling in my chest.

"I know it's not natural, but that's the point. I love Hettie very much, but this is bigger than her. Bigger than us. I found a way to break the limits of magic and science! We could be at the dawn of something new and you could help me change the world if you weren't always trying to stop me."

"I loved her too, but–"

"She's coming back. You don't have to speak about her like she's gone."

"Julius–"

"Don't you want her back? Don't you think there are plenty of people out there who want their loved ones back?"

"Of course I would love to see my cousin again, but–" She pauses. The leather of her gloves squeaks while she wrings her hands.

"But what? We don't have to stick to the old ways. We could advance, learn more, help people—"

"It's not right, and I'm just not sure you're really doing this for her."

Without the whirring of the machinery, silence spreads throughout the room like ink in water. I don't know how to respond. If any words could possibly fit with hers.

"I've made sure the sun and moon will be perfectly aligned. I found the best sample of every ingredient. I've worked hard on this for years. Why else would I be doing all this?"

She sighs, "You talk about helping people and furthering society, but I think we both know how famous this discovery would make you and how much money you'd get. If it even works in the first place. If we were meant to bring people back, don't you think it would be at least a little easier?"

At least she's not pretending anymore. "Look, I'm not trying to fight with you. Just give me the last ingredient and I'll be on my way," I say, wanting this conversation to end.

I watch as Sora's gaze wanders to the space under her bed. It's quick, but I notice, and she knows. Like lightning, she swipes her scythe blade from the grindstone and charges for me. I grab one of the bottles from my belt and launch it at her. It clanks against the blade and shatters on the wall, orange dust showering from above.

"Using old schoolyard alchemy on me, really? Can't even bring out the big guns?"

She's too fast and the space under the bed is full of boxes. I have to get to the secret storage underneath, but I'm wrenched away. Sora has grabbed my leg. I haphazardly take a box and fling it, making her release me. I reach for the chain attached to the blade, hoping she'll let go, but she's dragged along with it. We topple over each other until she's in front of the bed, guarding it. The scythe an extension of her.

"Please, Sora. You have to at least let me try." I try to get her to meet my gaze. She has the same golden-brown eyes as Hettie's though hers don't sparkle.

"Fine," she says, her heavy breathing matching my own. "But at least let me come with you."

"I can't put you in danger like that."

Sora stands, the blade of her scythe sliding into place behind her back. "Please, you're mistaken if you think I'm not going to go save my cousin."

She has a point. The plan was for me to go alone but if anyone has the right to come, it's her. Her eyes plead with me but I can also see defiance. I don't think she'll let me go alone no matter what I do. I nod in agreement. I'll have to apologize to Hettie later for bringing her cousin to such a dangerous place.

Sora moves to her dresser, pulling out a flask filled with a silvery liquid. The little trickster. "Besides, shadows are shifty. You need someone to watch your back. You need me."

I take one more sweeping look around the yard. It's only me, Sora, and the whistling wind. I've been dreading this moment. I've heard of the Deep many times in my life. The tales and myths speak of a dark, cold place no one can escape. But I'm going to try. I have to if I want to bring Hettie back.

I imagine what it will be like, the three of us emerging through the other side, triumphant. I throw open the portal. The wind changes direction, pulling us toward the black mass of swirls, almost matching the eclipse turning the sky red.

"Are you sure you want to come along? You can turn back now and–"

Sora trudges right through the portal, leaving me in the dust, or well, snow.

"Alrighty then."

I follow suit, albeit with not as much gusto. The tendrils of shadow enclose around me and for a few seconds, I can't breathe. The black fills every part of me until it spits me out into the other side.

Past the coughing and the tears in my eyes, I survey my surroundings. Sora catches her breath nearby. The lack of sound sends shivers down my spine, but what the area lacks in sound it makes up for with other senses. The air is thick, pressing down on me. From the way Sora's shoulders slump, I can tell it's affecting her as well.

"We need to move fast," I say between chokes. "We're not meant to be here in the first place."

I don't even think the shadows are meant to be here, as I can't sense any around us. Only a thin, rickety, extension bridge stretches ahead, leading into the black sky filled with mists of red. The same red of the bubbling liquid I find below when I peer over the cliff. It slinks and swirls around itself like wine. Through the fear, I can't help but feel satisfaction. It's all true, the stories I've collected from people, all the research I've done, it will all finally be worth it.

"Is this the way?" Sora asks, a slight tremble in her voice.

"This is what the legends say." I glance at my pocket watch. "But we need to hurry. Time moves faster here."

"Alright, let's go."

She waves her scythe ahead, prompting me to lead the way. The bridge creaks with every step, swaying side to side. I'm not sure how long we've been walking but I keep an eye on the time. I don't want to be trapped until the next eclipse.

Eventually, the bridge gives way to another cliffside. This one is bigger, and I stop in my tracks. Not because of the stone and black moss, but from the looming waterfall of red on the other side. The sound of the water rushing takes over, but I'm brought back to the present when I feel a hand on my shoulder. I wheel around to defend myself, but it's only Sora.

"Does that water seem different to you?"

I bite off a sarcastic response. Of course it looks different, it's red and bubbling, but I take a closer look. She's right, the liquid is moving upward, not down.

"What does that mean?" Sora asks.

"It means it's time." I move forward, but Sora holds me back.

"Maybe we shouldn't be here."

"It's okay." I give her shoulder a reassuring pat, but it doesn't seem to help.

"Julius, I'm serious, we shouldn't be here."

I can't help but sigh. I should've known she would keep trying to stop me.

"I can't quit now, not when I've come so far. You can stay back here if you want, but I need to do this. It will change everything."

I step ahead and bring out the container of thick purple oil. This is it. For five years I've traveled the world, fought all kinds of creatures and people, all for this moment. The water quiets as I approach, making it even more imposing somehow. Nevertheless, I take my chance, trying to remember the right words.

"I seek an audience with Henrietta Roas Tora."

The waterfall parts. Crystalline ice blue contrasts against the streams. I can hear Sora gasp behind me. There she is. Her entire body is wrapped in ice but I would recognize her anywhere. Her sleek black hair hangs around her, bangs framing her rounded face, and my heart skips a beat. It's been six years. More than half a decade since we skimmed over the lake for our task, since we both fell into the depths below. Since she saved me, only to leave me soon after.

It comes back to me then. The two of us on the lake together, everything peaceful. The clouds reflecting off the ice, making my Hettie appear as an angel gliding through the sky. Then the peace shattered, replaced by the chaos of creatures with razor-like tentacles tearing through the surface, pulling us in. The deep, dark cold taking over. The freedom of being released into the open air to the dreadful realization that she wasn't with me. It took me a year after she left to even attempt to bring her back and five more to achieve it, or so I hope.

"My beloved, is that you?"

She doesn't respond, but she looks peaceful with her eyes closed, black lashes against smooth skin. It's okay, I know it's really her. I sprint to her as my mind floods with ideas. There's so much we would need to catch up on. I could tell her all about my travels. When word gets out about what I've discovered, we could tour the world together. Everyone will want the recipe to our accomplishment. I could share it with the world and she could add her experience if she chose to. Families could be glued back together, lovers reunited. We would provide everyone with what was kept from them for so long.

The liquid lowers my Hettie down so we're eye-to-eye. Now that I'm closer, I can't help but feel like something is not quite right. But it doesn't matter, I still love her and we can make anything work.

My hands shake as I remove the cork from the flask. The cold reaches me before I can touch the ice flowing around us. The hairs on the back of my neck stand up, but besides the three of us there is no one around. I shove my fear away and pour the oily substance over the ice. The purple sludge wraps around it, steam rising as it melts. As it gives way, the substance finally reaches the person inside. A light emanates from within.

I've done it. "Hettie, can you hear me?"

No answer. Something is wrong. The light grows darker, becoming shadow as her figure turns to dust. I try to reach for her, but she slips through my fingers until there's nothing left.

"Wait…come back…please."

"You must really believe you're more powerful than you are," a voice says from nowhere, making me jump.

"W-who is that?" I call. The cliff face is empty save for Sora, who stands guard, waiting for the potential attacker.

"Did you think you could disrupt the balance of things and elude the consequences?" The voice gets closer and though I can't sense a presence, the chill from the ice sinks deeper, pouring into me. I stagger back and Sora calls out, but something is keeping her from reaching my section of rock.

"Why are you doing this?" I whisper, my breath slowing. I still can't sense anything.

"I see you're still demanding things. You were lucky. She helped you escape the ice once, but now it will be a part of you always."

That's when it hits me. The booming voice, the threats. Everywhere I've visited trying to learn about this place, they all have their stories. Tales of mysterious shadows guarding the ones who come here, doing anything to assure their safety. But most importantly, they always dole out punishments when rules are broken. I should've known this was going to happen, but I wouldn't have gotten this far if I had let anyone stop me.

Any warmth I had leaves me and I can feel every beat of my heart. It feels like stone. I fall to my knees, not caring if the voice is still around. I can't imagine it could do any more damage than it already has.

"Julius, what's going on, are you okay?" Sora's voice is far away like she's trying to speak underwater.

The bridge behind us shakes, the panels beginning to fall away.

"We need to go." She doesn't wait for a response, pulling me from the ground. I let her drag me along, I can't seem to find the will to do anything, like a part of me is gone. The wood splinters behind us, biting at our heels like a hungry dog.

"Wait, can you make another portal?"

She's still so far away. How did she get so far?

"C'mon, help me. Do you really want to be stuck in this place?"

Her words pull my mind from the numbness. This is all my fault. I'm the reason Sora's here. I may not have been able to bring Hettie back, but Sora is her family. I can't drag her down with me. I try to call the portal open, but I can't find the strength. Good thing I always bring a backup. I reach for the bottle, a blue wind raging from inside. I throw it and it shatters, but before the portal can fully form, the bottle tumbles into the void below.

I almost give up right there. This is what I deserve after all, but out of the corner of my eye, I see it. A twisting vortex of blue light floating below the bridge, just ahead.

"Sora, we have to jump," I call out, but she's already moving, pulling at my collar. A small part of me wishes she'd leave me behind, but I can't hurt her more than I already have. The weight of the air presses down harder and harder as we plummet into the depths. I feel the blue wind whip around us, blowing strands of hair in my face. I close my eyes and don't open them again until I feel the snow envelop me.

"Julius, are you alright? Say something."

Sora's voice is distant once more, taking on a watery sound. I sink deeper into the snow, trying to avoid the memories that rush at me from everywhere. All my work, five years of it, all for nothing.

"Do you need help?"

Sora. The closest thing I have left to family. It will never be made official though. Even if it was possible, I don't think she'd want to be associated with me. I've put her in danger and for what? Magical and scientific achievement? Attempting something I should've known was impossible? I curl into a ball, sinking deeper into the snow. Strange, it doesn't feel so cold anymore.

"Good, you're alive. Let's go."

After I don't respond, I feel her draw me into a sitting position. Her eyes meet mine, I have to look away.

"Don't make me carry you, I promise it won't be fun."

"I'm so sorry, Sora. I truly thought I could do it, but all I did was endanger you. If you want to leave me out here and head back home, I understand."

I still can't manage to look at her face, but her shadow on the white expanse stands rigid, hands on its hips.

"Do you really think I would leave you out here?"

"It's what I deserve. I'm not fully sure what they did, but it's taken something away from me and I brought it on myself."

The snow crunches as Sora crouches beside me.

"Besides, I don't really know what's left for me to do. I couldn't bring Hettie back, I could barely open a portal. Maybe I don't have a use anymore."

For a while, there's nothing but the sound of the wind whistling around us. The red in the sky has started to fade away, but there are remnants of pink clouds. Eventually, Sora breaks the quiet.

"I know you wanted her back, I did too, but even though she's not here. Do you really think she'd want you to quit?"

That's surprising. I expected her to get angry with me, maybe throw something. I wouldn't blame her, I'd even encourage it.

"And do you really think she'd want to see you down in the snow, pitying yourself?"

I can't help but chuckle, at least I can still laugh. "Not likely."

"There are other ways to solve the mysteries of the world, even without some unknown power somewhere. You're one of the most foolish, yet smartest people I know. You'll find another purpose, Julius."

I nod, but can't find any words to say.

"Can you promise me you won't give up? If not for yourself or for me, then for my cousin? For the people your discoveries could help someday?"

I want to, really, deep down, but something isn't right. The part of me that wants to keep Sora's promise feels constricted, frozen. She makes me look straight at her now, awaiting an answer.

"I promise." And I want to mean it. I will mean it. Whatever changed in me, I'll fix it. After I'm back to normal, I'll do all kinds of things, not only for myself but for the world as well. The ambition fades a little, trapped by invisible ice, but it never fully leaves. I need to keep it safe so it never will.

Sora stands once more, lifting me up. "Okay then, it's a deal. Now let's get home, I'm hungry."

"Alright," I laugh, "let's go home."

A Fossil of Proportion

First Published in 2021 on RebeccaMZornow.com

Rebecca M. Zornow

Candace estimated the cost of the simple drive was equivalent to a small country's GDP. The rover's price tag was $2.5 billion to build, and then another $3 billion to transport from Earth. The fuel she couldn't guess at, but it sure wasn't produced on-planet. She knew the soldiers around her made half a million dollars a year—in the midst of packing and boarding, Candace had found the time to look the figure up. All the humans, Candace included, cost much more than the rover to transport because of the complexity of the chemical brew it took to ice a human body for the four-year trip.

As an academic, Candace was probably the lowest ticket item on the ride.

Hot air blew past her ears. The rover was open on top but, unlike the simple frames used on moons and planets with thin atmospheres, this one had a windshield. And needed it. Dust accumulated in the crease of her neck and her hair felt thick with it.

Her left arm tremored slightly. Medical told her that morning it was the effects of cryosleep still wearing off. Candace disregarded the assessment, not from lack of respect to the staff, but only because she knew her flaws. When she got nervous, her arms twitched like a short-circuiting Robotx.

It struck her that she was higher paid than her assistants. The thought bolstered her.

On her right, Izaak adjusted his nasal cannula again; perhaps she wasn't the only nervous one.

Noticing Izaak's clear plastic tube made her recall her own. It was like any uncomfortable item of clothing—after a while, you forgot about it, but any small reminder made it itch and pinch. The difference was, if you dumped the accessory in this troposphere, your face would slowly turn blue.

"I suggest you leave it alone, ma'am." The soldier—he never offered his name—nodded at her hand, adjusting the nasal cannula without her realizing it.

Candace lowered the offending hand. "Sorry. I bet they cost more than my house back home."

The soldier gave her a blank look. "No, ma'am—"

"Doctor," Izaak corrected.

"—it's just you never get used to wearing it." The soldier directed his focus ahead, over the shoulder of the driver.

"Do we have far to go?" Candace asked.

"No, ma'am," he said, peering at a screen on the dashboard. "Three-point-two clicks."

Izaak attempted to draw their guide into conversation, but it fizzled, and all four travelers directed their gaze at the bleak horizon.

It rankled Candace that Lanna was back at the base. Lanna *was* having difficulty adjusting from the long stint in cryosleep. She couldn't keep dried food down, couldn't yet keep tea or water down, hadn't yet passed any liquids from her body. Lanna was furious to be tied to an IV and catheter on what she claimed was the most important day of her career. Candace had to agree, though privately thought it'd be a poor experience no matter the workday in question.

Surely Lanna would feel better soon, but she was the one on the paleontology team most elated by the sheer thrill of traveling to a faraway planet. That wasn't quite fair, Candace considered. She was excited to be here too—to dig.

It wasn't a bad appointment, all things considered. Minas Grant was a trifle hot—40.5° C at the moment—and the supplementary oxygen was a nuisance, but she could have been sent to Chiang T where she'd be swathed in a head-to-toe space suit every waking minute. Eyes closed, the hot weather made her feel she was vacationing somewhere tropical, but dry.

The weather was good for one other thing: preservation.

Candace watched the rocky, barren terrain roll by, composing in her head how to describe it to her nephews in the video message she'd send later, until the rover came to an abrupt stop. The two soldiers were out before the dust settled. Izaak and Candace had difficulty maneuvering the oxygen tanks to their backs and paused to check the plastic cords that ran from their noses to the tanks.

The soldiers stood casually while they waited, a faint buzz of amusement radiating off them.

Izaak unloaded two small packs and handed one to Candace. She turned to the soldiers, expectantly.

"We have to walk from here. It's not far, just the bottom of this ridge. The footing's best over there." He pointed east and Candace spotted a twisted incline.

She took a deep breath, trying to ignore the wet circles already forming under her arms, and started out. Exotic location aside, it felt like so many other digs in her life—a farmer pointing toward churned earth, a biologist sketching a map, a child pointing where she saw "dem bones".

The soldiers quickly took the lead, leaving Candace and Izaak to struggle with their air tanks and heavy packs. Candace supposed it was fair; the soldiers carried air tanks and their guns.

The resulting thought struck Candace so suddenly she interrupted Izaak's speculation about the soil, which was a truly brittle layer of sedimentary rock.

"Why do you think they carry guns?"

Izaak glanced ahead at the soldiers, unconcerned. "What else are they supposed to do? Getting to lug those things around is part of the reason they signed up." He mopped his brow with his bare hand, but the sweat only smeared. Still, he smiled. "Just like I had dreams of lugging metal chisels through 100-degree weather."

"But there's nobody else here," Candace pressed on. "If you get to bring one thing to a deserted island with no one on it, you don't choose a weapon, you choose a tool."

Izaak shrugged. "Even deserted islands have wild boars."

The steep incline forced them to stop talking and mind their footing. When Candace got her breath back, she continued her train of thought. "Well," it came out clipped, "if they're supposed to be protecting us, they could at least give their names."

"Nah, Candace, don't worry. I saw the reports too." He hoisted his pack up higher. "There's nothing out here. Guns are just a habit for them."

They neared the soldiers—Candace couldn't help but think of them as guards—and Izaak asked how long they'd been on-planet.

"Eight months. Eight Earth-months," the driver clarified.

The other didn't offer an answer, but turned and said, "It's just through here."

It was clear why they parked the rover where they did. While most of the drive from the military base was flat and the hike ran down a relatively stable incline, the end destination was a mammoth gully. Candace didn't think it could be properly classified as a canyon, but it was definitely a valley. She muttered while wondering if it was a long-dried-out riverbed or if the chasm was the result of geological activity.

There was much to learn about Minas Grant. By this point, plenty of rock and mineral samples had made their way back to Earth—Candace referenced a few in the dissertation she wrote way back when she woke pain-free in the morning—but her team was the first independent archaeology expedition to come. Until this point, only Space Force had explored, colonized, and, to a lesser extent, studied Minas Grant.

And she was there for good reason.

Candace walked, eyes on the dried and cracked ground, when she bumped hard into Mr. No Name Soldier. The bag of metal tools pulled her off balance and she fell haphazardly on top of the canvas sack.

"Are you alright, Ms. Shah?"

"Dr. Shah," Izaak corrected, helping Candace up by the arm.

She set to beating the dust off her clothes as Izaak double checked the plastic tube connected to her tank. His biggest worry with interstellar travel was not the ship blowing up at launch or never waking from a frozen sleep, but that he was going to a planet with only 18% oxygen in its atmosphere. He had memorized the simple air tank manual and quizzed Candace at breakfast.

As Izaak and Candace grumbled and fussed with their bags and tanks, it struck her that the two soldiers went quiet. Candace looked up quickly and vertigo swept through her body, leaving her hands shaky. Izaak saw her expression and followed her gaze.

"Is that…"

"We're hoping you can tell us what 'that' is, ma'am."

Over Candace's head, over everyone's head, stood the stark red cliff face lined with flakey rock and sediment. A protrusion of much lighter sand-colored fossils breached the face of the stone. The organic material, long turned to rock, lay in a pattern that Candace recognized as the skeletal hallmark of every Earth mammal, reptile, fish, bird, and amphibian.

Ribs.

Ribs the size of a giant.

Candace's mind spun as it tried to reconcile this information with its known understanding of the universe. They couldn't be rib bones. They just couldn't. They were much too large, for one thing—bigger than the dinosaur bones the founders of paleontology studied. It must be a trick of perspective, the bones of some ancient alien species scattered randomly, and Candace's mind was simply filling in the gaps.

The brief was vague, but Dr. Candace R. Shah had assumed, a bit smugly, that the military brain that compiled the document was entirely unequipped and untrained to write about potential excavation sites. Candace assumed she was coming to analyze the fossils of single-celled organisms or something alien, something entirely unseen.

She was shocked to recognize the bones of Earth, lightyears away and several times larger.

Her unease was palatable to the others.

The driver cleared his throat and looked back toward the rocky path. "There's good daylight for seven hours yet. We'll come for you then. Dr. Shah?" he said, trying to make his directive sound like a question.

Izaak was the first to recover. "Sure," he said, glancing down at the small pack he brought, "but don't expect us to make much progress today."

Like all dig sites Candace had ever worked on, they started with the most useful and technologically appropriate tool: a spool of string. After mapping out a grid with string wrapped around sticks at one-meter intervals, Candace sketched the layout on her tablet. Because the dig site was on the edge of the cliff, they had to map out two sides. Every excavation was 3-D by nature, but they didn't usually threaten to collapse out one side.

Only part of the larger skeleton showed—ribs 9, 10, and 11 if the speculation of Candace's mind could be trusted. Little rib number 12 was still hidden under the rock, her inner dialogue whispered.

Over the next eight weeks, weeks being 5.4 Earth days, Candace and her team blasted their way strategically through rock with dynamite until it was feasible for Lanna, who was on site as soon as untethered, to jackhammer rock away. They all took turns scanning the broken rock for any interesting sample or specimen, and then carting it from the site in a wheelbarrow.

Lanna's infectious enthusiasm roped the driver and his pal into the work. They only gave up their names—Privates Nguyen and Winter, respectively— when Lanna took to calling them Captain Driver and General Stands-a-lot.

Private Nguyen had laughed at the low-tech nature of the paleontologists' work but pulled strings to get a specialized vehicle for the hauling. They removed tons of rock from the dig site, but within the frame of the huge valley, their impact was tiny.

Still, the ribs—Candace couldn't think of them any other way—were uncovered little by little until they protruded so much one could stand inside them like a half-formed cavern.

Usually, Candace was full of anticipation and excitement when the more refined stages of excavation started. Instead, she felt a wet, dark knot in her stomach.

Izaak and Lanna had discussed the merits of starting on top of the cliff, working their way down.

"No, we'll start in the valley, go inwards."

Lanna looked at Candace with surprise, her button nose turned up. "But that's going to destabilize the top layer. The fossils will break if we pull the carpet out from under them."

Candace nodded as if she was considering Lanna's point. "We won't come at it from that direction for long, just enough to determine the placement and orientation of the skeleton. I don't want to spend our time taking this cliff apart layer by layer if what we want is indeed on the edge, literally jutting out at us."

Izaak nodded his agreement and Candace left the rest of her curiosity unvoiced. Before they went any further, she needed to get a better sense of the skeleton's shape, yes, but more than that, she needed to know if there was a sternum, if the skeleton was inherently similar to the ones found on Earth— and if so, what that might mean.

They made great progress after that. Not only did the ribs stand out, they uncovered the tip of a pelvic bone and roughed out the shape of an arm bone, detached and strewn aside by time.

The appearance of the pelvic bone lifted the existential dread from Candace's shoulders. From what they uncovered of the ilium so far, she knew it wasn't the hollow scoop of a mammalian skeleton, wide enough to birth living young. Instead, it was shallow and narrow, much more reptilian in nature.

Each day, Candace scaled the scaffolding to assess the previous day's progress. It unnerved her when the group arrived to find things exactly as left each night. No animal came to nose through their supplies, and they had yet to have a good rainfall. Even the canvas and tarps hardly shifted in the mild wind. Candace had expected excavation on Minas Grant to feel different. She just didn't expect it to feel dead.

The cry came at midafternoon. Candace was at an upper level of the scaffolding, diving through rock to determine if the rib-like protrusions joined at a spine, the supposedly prized gift of Mother Earth.

Lanna and Izaak were lower, hoping to dig deep enough to excavate a bone fragment so they could remove and wrap it in preparation for lab work.

The cry alarmed Candace, but there was no deathly shifting of rock or the cursing that followed breakage of a delicate piece.

"What is it?" she called down.

There were words, but no clear answer. Candace stuck her head over the platform side and saw Izaak, hands covering his mouth. Lanna had her own mouth open with glee.

"What's going on?" Candace repeated, but she was already down the steps, jumping two at a time.

Lanna, speechless, pointed at the cliff face. A small, smooth expanse of fossilized bone showed through the rock. This one on a much smaller scale than they'd been working with. The shape was rounded and demonstrated clear, hauntingly familiar depressions. And a row of teeth.

The skull smiled back, and Candace recoiled.

"You see it too," Izaak said weakly. It wasn't a question. He saw the tension in Candace's body "It's clearly not part of the larger skeleton. The giant beast, it—"

"Ate this person," Lanna finished eagerly.

Candace pieced together what they were looking at, though she resisted the conclusion on a cellular level. "And then Specimen One died soon after and both skeletons were fossilized." She sounded strangely formal to her own ears.

"Is it human?" Lanna asked.

A harsh laugh burst from Candace. "Of course not, Lanna. It's eerily familiar, but…an echo, that's all. Let's not speculate."

Lanna was incredulous. "Winter and Nguyen are going to notice. It stands out like a face in a photograph."

Lanna was right, Candace thought. It was a bit like seeing yourself in a large picture. No matter how busy or big, your own face would stick out within seconds. Anyone who saw these fossils would speculate.

Candace said quickly, "We need to cover it. This isn't—well, this will be massively misunderstood."

Three of the four heads turned at the sound of rock crunching underfoot on the meager pathway. Voices carried through the chasm and Candace raced for a measure of tarp. She seized it from their table of haphazard supplies and rushed to drape it over the smaller fossil—she couldn't think of it as a human head.

She had pounded in a single, thin peg when visitors arrived. Her shirt was already damp with sweat, but she felt a fresh trickle down her back.

Private Winter led the oncoming group into the valley, Private Nguyen bringing up the rear. Both were clearly on their best behavior, no dawdling gate or casual stance. The members of the small group they escorted were dressed in uniform and Candace knew instantly by their carriage that they were important.

"Dr. Shah," a woman called. "We've come to view your little dig. Though it's not as little as perhaps you expected."

As the woman drew closer, pock marks sprung out on her visage. Although the skin underneath the marks glowed with health, Candace had trouble placing the woman's age.

"General Fisher," the woman said by way of introduction.

Candace smiled weakly. "Yes, it's quite big indeed." She descended the scaffolding, trying to ignore the shakes in her arm. "Come, let's start at the top. I'll explain it layer by layer."

"No need, Doctor. We came that way and Private Winter explained what you told him, in a rudimentary way, I'm sure." The general's words were polite enough but carried an edge of patronization. The others spread out to look around with an air of afternoon picnicking. Candace felt control of the dig slipping through her fingers. General Fisher was in charge.

There was nothing to be done as the visitors ascended the scaffolding like a flock of tourists. Candace bit back repeated reminders not to touch or scratch at the rock like a badger, but only because Izaak did it for her.

"Oh, I'd leave that alone, it's very delicate—"

But it was too late. A member of the party lifted the tarp and stood suddenly erect. Candace knew what he saw, what he was processing.

And they were completely ridiculous thoughts. What would a fossilized skull from a member of the genus Homo be doing here on Minas Grant? This was not the bleached bone of desert exposure. This was a true fossil, one Candace couldn't wait to have undergo radioactive dating, but it was far too old to be a modern human.

The others crowded around as they discussed the finding in earnest, but Candace stood apart. She wasn't going to make claims or concessions regarding an in-progress dig site, as much as she was prompted to. She felt General Fisher's eyes on her, assessing her reticent attitude.

"Private Nguyen," the General finally said. The private snapped to attention. "We're ready to go back. Private Winter, guard this site. Don't let anything happen to that skull. And Dr. Shah," General Fisher called over her shoulder, "keep digging. But carefully. If any of this breaks, you may just be out of a ride home."

The Candace of the past was happiest at site working to excavate the next mystery, a new piece of her own planet's history. But weeks into the Minas Grant dig, she just wanted to go home. Crawl back in that damned freezer and fly to Earth. See her nephews, eat something that grew in the dirt, and sleep in her condo surrounded by the buzz of a living city. Shoot. She forgot she sold the condo. If the people she sold to were still the owners, they had already lived on sunny Lilac Drive for four years, not the few months it seemed to Candace. There was no running away.

Instead, Candace, Lanna, and Izaak worked 14-hour days in a 20-hour day cycle trying to uncover "Larry," as Lanna dubbed the giant lizard body (named after herself), and "Izzy," the humanoid skeleton (named after Izaak). Izzy was out of the ground and temporarily relocated back to the base, waiting for further work. Larry was as monstrous as ever, only giving up his secrets week by week.

On rare days off, troops drove out to climb over the dig site, the only tourist attraction on Minas Grant. It was a huge project for three paleontologists, especially if one person had to dedicate their time to telling off gawking soldiers. Still, the commands from General Fisher, relayed via Private Winter, were to work harder and longer to the point that they had to bring two tanks each to the site. They'd otherwise run out of supplemental oxygen during their shift. Every morning, Candace saw Izaak double check that the tanks were at full capacity.

Candace felt more and more like a slave than a visiting scientist, which was why she found herself in a storage shed well past midnight; midnight being entirely relative on a planet with only twenty hours in a day.

The crates were well organized—it was the military, not a volunteer-sponsored dig—and in the dark, the warehouse felt endless. Candace was there on a hunch.

That skull, Izzy's creepy, broken, beaming smile, smashed Candace's brain when she first saw it. What a fossilized human-like skull was doing four lightyears from Earth, when all of human history had worked its collective butt off trying to reach the stars just decades earlier, was beyond Candace.

Over the weeks, Candace obsessed over the skull. It was out of her hands all too quickly. Then all she could do was reflect on how General Fisher didn't seem surprised at all when the skull was revealed.

Which told Candace General Fisher had ideas, theories, and potentially knowledge.

Candace wanted that knowledge.

Candice sniffed at another crate full of rocks. She replaced the lid the best she could without hammering it shut—science forgive her if it shifted in flight and smashed open, destroying all the samples inside. The echoes of her movement carried through the factory. She couldn't risk the pounding noise. She felt as jittery as an airscribe.

She scratched at the now-red patch under the nasal cannula and shifted to another row of shelves.

A light flickered overhead, and Candace crouched down, dropping her flashlight.

"It's over two more, Dr. Shah."

Candace looked up and opened her mouth to explain what she was doing when the stern general made her appearance from the endless rows. "Can it, Shah. Follow me."

Candace stood heavily from her crouch, air tank swaying on her back, and did just that. Her mind raced as she considered what her punishment might be. No, she was a scientist looking for a sample. The whole reason they had brought her was for her mind. How could she be punished for putting it to work?

The general held her hand out for the crowbar. Candace handed it over and watched as General Fisher pried open a crate.

The general pulled aside packing material. Inside was a hard-shelled case. Once opened, it revealed a sample nestled in soft foam. General Fisher threw the crowbar to the ground, making Candace wince away from the harsh clatter of metal on concrete. General Fisher gingerly lifted a flat brown mass of fossilized stone.

"That's not Izzy."

General Fisher looked warily at Candace; eyes dark in her pock-marked face.

"The, uh, skull. We named the skull," Candace said quietly.

"You think the skull blew your mind? Wait until you see this. While I digging the site for the reactor, we've found dozens of bones, but only one of these."

"Fossils," Candace corrected. "The bones themselves are not preserved, only their shadow."

"Quite." There was a note of resigned amusement in General Fisher's voice.

Candace leaned over the browned rock. She drew back with a breath. "A techno fossil."

The fossil was not the impression of wood or bone or even fibrous plants. It was a *made* thing. A technologically advanced thing. Candace felt breathless as the conclusion thrummed inside her head.

"This isn't the first time the military has come to this planet."

General Fisher's hard face was impassive, concealing some immense vulnerability. "So, you think it's a weapon too?" she asked softly.

Candace ignored her and finished her thought. "It's not the first time the military came to this planet, but it's the first time for our military." Her voice broke to a whisper. "A civilization, like ours, here and gone."

General Fisher nodded, looking at the fossil with disdain. "We're not the great expansion humanity dreamed of. This is the end of our story. *We* are the end of the story. Humanity once settled across the universe, but there was a failure to thrive." Life bled from the General's face as she spoke. "A whimper, not a bang."

Dr. Shah fixed General Fisher with a stare, realizing for the first time, *she* was the professional there. She spoke with compassion, but more than a little authority.

"That feeling you're having—that it's all over before you even knew it started? That's what I specialize in."

Moon Walk

Don Brittnacher

In July of 1969, I was a teenager living and working on a dairy farm, when we first walked on the moon. I say "we", because I think most Americans felt like they were up there too.

While we were haying in the middle of the afternoon, the lunar module landed on the moon. "The Eagle has landed," came the transmission to earth. The United States was in a race with the Soviet Union for bragging rights to the moon. At the same time, Wisconsin dairymen were in a race against the weather to cut, dry, harvest, and store enough feed so their livestock would survive the winter. While the broad backs of the farm laborers sweated in the fields and hay mows, our astronauts sweated in their spacesuits.

It wasn't that the American farmer was disinterested in things skyward. Farmers in the American heartland were acutely aware of signs in the sky of pending weather. The universe of the Wisconsin dairy farmer extended across his 120 acres, and up to the clouds. The farmer glanced to the heavens as often as he inspected his earth and crops. Winds out of the east meant rain. Thunderclouds on the western horizon provided two hours to finish fieldwork, depending on their speed. Cloudless nights in winter meant bitter cold mornings, requiring heat tape on water pipes and plugging in the engine warmers on tractors.

A few followed the traditions of the old country, and focused their thoughts on the sky for other reasons. They paused their work in the fields at the sound of the distant church bells at noon, looked upward, and murmured the words of the Angelus, asking the Almighty's angels to watch over their crops.

But the moon? How does it affect calf birthing, milk prices, or corn wilt? Most farmers were too busy to contemplate anything other than raising crops and cows, and providing good milk to the dairy. We weren't interested in the planets and solar system; there wasn't time for that.

On July 20, 1969, the summer day stretched from the 5:00 a.m. milking to the 8:30 p.m. calf feeding, with the morning and evening milkings separated by non-stop work in the sun. I came in from late barn chores, showered in the basement, and went upstairs, passing the television set on my way to grab a bowl of ice cream. I found myself mesmerized by the grainy images on the screen.

The small kitchen TV usually provided us with farm news during mealtime, but that night it was describing preparations for the spacewalk. I was too young to fully understand the worldwide significance of the lunar landing, but I knew it was important to me. I was the one on the farm who read books, while other kids tinkered with car engines. Dairying taught me important life lessons about birth and death, loyalty to family, hard work, and self-reliance. But, late at night, lying in my bed, I dreamt of other things. The images on the TV screen underscored that a wider world awaited me off the farm.

The rest of the family turned in for the night at 9:00, but my eyes were glued to the set. I listened as Walter Cronkite described the lunar walk procedure, dressing for the moon's atmosphere, opening the hatch, and descending the skinny ladder to the moon's surface. At 10:00 midwestern time, half a billion people around the world heard Neil Armstrong say, "That's one small step for man, one giant leap for mankind." As those words reverberated across time zones, the only sound heard in most midwestern dairy households was the gentle snoring of farmers deep in sleep, resting for the routine of the next long day.

I remained motionless at the kitchen table till around 2:00 the next morning, watching history unfold. The view of the activities on the moon, so foreign to my world of cows and crops, was intoxicating. I wasn't so much drawn to the life of the astronaut as I was feeling unmoored from the world of dairy farming. The thought was unsettling, yet freeing. As I went to bed, I didn't know where I belonged, but I felt a quiet excitement in knowing that opportunities were waiting for me to explore.

SMITHworks Writing Group

The SMITHworks Writing Group is a part of the creative programming at the Elisha D. Smith Public Library in Menasha, WI.

The group was founded in February 2022 as a way for local writers to enhance their writing craft, learn about the publishing industry, and connect with other writers.

They currently meet on the second Monday of the month at 6:30 PM under the leadership of facilitator Rebecca M. Zornow.

Unmapped: An Anthology is their second collection.

Since its founding in 1896 as a community reading room, the Elisha D. Smith Public Library has sought to provide its community members with the resources they need to achieve their goals. Over the course of the last 125 years, those resources have evolved. The original quiet reading room now shares space with active learning and community engagement spaces. The original book collection has grown to include movies, audiobooks, games, puzzles, tools, and electronics. The cumbersome, but beloved, card catalog has given way to computer access from anywhere, at any time.

So much more than books, the Elisha D. Smith Library provides our community with knowledge, new skills, and connections. It's open to everyone in the community and is a place to explore, connect, and create. It's a library of a new era, a living and functional meeting place open to all.

The Elisha D. Smith Public Library is driven by our community. Meet friends, read, develop new skills, create, and relax. Visit with family, book a meeting room, or spend a workday here. Our team and resources are here for the community. Connect with the Elisha D. Smith Public Library at MenashaLibrary.org

Conquer Books was founded by authors and book coaches Nicole Van Den Eng and Rebecca M. Zornow. They coach writers who struggle to craft their inner magic into words. At Conquer Books, their job is to transform budding writers into dynamic professionals, and wild ideas into powerful books.

As speculative fiction fanatics, they know the world is hungry for stories that span universes and want to help bring yours to life.

Sign up for their newsletter and get the free guide "25 Questions to Ask your Manuscript" at ConquerBooks.com.